T0103854

Bargain for MURDER

Nick Kleve

Order this book online at www.trafford.com
or email orders@trafford.com

Most Trafford titles are also available at major online book retailers.

© Copyright 2014 Nick Kleve.
All rights reserved. No part of this publication may be reproduced,
stored in a retrieval system, or transmitted, in any form or by
any means, electronic, mechanical, photocopying, recording, or
otherwise, without the written prior permission of the author.

Printed in the United States of America.

ISBN: 978-1-4907-1801-9 (sc)
ISBN: 978-1-4907-1800-2 (e)

Because of the dynamic nature of the Internet, any web addresses or
links contained in this book may have changed since publication and
may no longer be valid. The views expressed in this work are solely those
of the author and do not necessarily reflect the views of the publisher,
and the publisher hereby disclaims any responsibility for them.

Any people depicted in stock imagery provided by Thinkstock are models,
and such images are being used for illustrative purposes only.
Certain stock imagery © Thinkstock.

Trafford rev. 02/06/2014

 **Trafford** www.trafford.com
PUBLISHING
North America & international
toll-free: 1 888 232 4444 (USA & Canada)
fax: 812 355 4082

RED DRIPS FROM MY CHIN WHERE I HAVE
BEEN EATING.
NOT ALL THE BLOOD, NO WHERE NEAR ALL,
IS WIPED OFF MY MOUTH
CLOTS OF RED MESS MY HAIR,
AND THE TIGER, AND BUFFALO, KNOW HOW.
YES, I AM A KILLER.
I COME FROM KILLING.
I GO TO MORE.

CARL SANDBURG

CHAPTER 1

A Chicago Suburb

George Harwood had the covers pulled up over his head like a little boy afraid of the dark, only it wasn't night and it wasn't dark. It was the crack of dawn, and the moment one single ray, just one single beam of light, peeked through his window, his eyes jumped wide awake as if someone had blown a trumpet for reveille. He tried everything to keep from waking so early but nothing seemed to work. Even the double insulated drapes that he had purchased form the understanding and confident young salesclerk at Marshall Field's, hadn't done the job sufficiently enough to keep the light form filtering through. So he lay, wide awake. It was no use. The sun had won again. Surrendering he threw back the covers and sat up.

Then it struck him. It was completely quiet outside. Honest to God quiet. The rain and wind the city of Chicago had experienced for the last four days had finally stopped. Wind gusts of up to seventy miles per hour had been reported and enough rain had fallen to cause major flooding and more serious than that, a doubleheader at Wrigley field had to be canceled.

To the Chicagoans, the Cubs ranked in importance somewhere between breathing, eating regularly and good sex.

But for now at least it seemed like the rain finally stopped. He reluctantly got out of bed and walked over to the cherry antique rocker that had been a gift form his grandmother. The rocker had sat for many years in the corner of his bedrooms like a sentry on duty. He had it with him since his childhood and wherever he went so did it. His running shorts, shirt, socks and shoes were sprawled about it just where he had left the morning before the rains began. He quickly got dressed and walked down the hall to the kitchen. Once in the kitchen, he turned on the small Sony TV that sat next to his Vita master blender on the kitchen counter. While he listened to the morning news announcer, he walked over to the refrigerator and removed orange juice, wheat germ, one egg and a pint of Dannon plain yogurt.

"The stationary front that has plagued our area for the last four days has finally moved east." The commentator said in his deep professional sounding voice. "Many homes a business are still without electricity. County Officials still advise that it may be necessary to continue boiling water until water supplies can be checked for contamination. Many underpasses are still flooded. Travel is hazardous and police are advising that you remain at home until the water has had a chance to subside".

He emphasized the words, "remain at home".

George threw all of the ingredients into the blender and then sat down on one of the study modern kitchen chairs. He pulled up his socks and slipped on his well used and soiled Reeboks taking care to tie them securely. When he finished he walked over to the cabinet next to the refrigerator and took out an assortment of vitamins and minerals. Uncapped them, he took a colorful pill from each one and downed them with his orange shaded liquid breakfast. He went out the side door of the house and walked into an almost awe inspiring completed sunrise.

He stretched his leg muscles while leaning against the siding of the old frame house that had once belonged to his parents. He had spent mort of his young life here and loved it. Only college and a career in advertising forced him away. But when his parents died in an auto wreck four years earlier and left the house to him he decided to leave his high rise, high-rent apartment downtown and move back here. He hadn't regretted his decision once.

He started to jog down the street on his usual morning route. massive oak and elm trees lined the streets on both sides. Steady raindrops fell from heavily over-loaded leaves. Birds sang louder and more cheerful than ever. He felt it was going to be a glorious day.

It was not unusual for him to run five miles through his old neighborhood but because it was such a beautiful morning and it felt so good to be out in the fresh air again he thought he might double that and run ten instead.

When his mother and father lived here the area was mostly occupied by upper class wasps. Then as the years went by, as with older neighborhoods, it began to crumble. The Wasps left in search of more modern and manicured areas with names like Rolling Hills and Hidden Valley, and with houses that looked as much alike as plastic pieces on a Monopoly board. When he moved here three years ago, a change began taking place. The Yuppies began buying up the quaint, moderately price older homes and expensive and time consuming refurbishing started taking place everywhere. The beauty was slowly returning. Now most of the cars that sat in the narrow driveways cost more than the actual purchase price of the house they belonged to.

He smiled with deepened pride at the pleasant surroundings as he jogged well into his third mile. The next leg of his route took him along the almost completely abandoned industrial area that paralleled the old railroad tracks. Productivity there disappeared along with those mile long freight trains and the area became bleak and empty. According to an article in a local newspaper the property had been purchased by a Canadian conglomerate and plans were being drawn up for a shopping mall to service the affluent baby boomers that invaded the area. He stopped at the corner of Maple and Lee streets waiting for the light to change while jogging in place. Across the street he could see a few houses that had been transformed into better condition than their original owners could have ever envisioned. Small glass windows had been replaced by panoramic bays or romantic French doors. The old traditional white siding had been changed with either redwood siding, stone or brick. The only thing missing to make them picture perfect were the picket fences and brilliant rose gardens in full bloom to surround them. Then again, it was too early in the year for that, but somehow George felt they would be there eventually and the picture would be complete.

A sudden noise caught his attention. He looked in the direction of the distraction and could see a gray van barreling down the street towards him, well over the 35 mile per hour posted speed. As it came closer he saw too late the large dark puddle of water at the side of the curb just in front of him. He tried to back up shielding his face with his hands from the gush of water that was to cover his body. But his actions were too late and he received a complete soaking as the van roared past him. When he uncovered his hands and looked down at his drenched white running suite he began to scream, and scream. He screamed until people stopped what they were doing and came out of their houses to see what all the racket was about.

CHAPTER 2

Squad cars blocked the intersection at Maple and Lee Streets on all sides. Numerous red lights flashed erratically as twinkling on a Christmas tree. People from the neighborhood and curious strangers alike stood behind the barricades of yellow crime ribbons trying to get a better look at what all the excitement was about. A dark unmarked car pulled up to the curb. The driver, who was black and about 5'10", was short in comparison to his partner, who towered well over six feet. The tall man's lanky body seemed to uncoil as he exited the car on the passenger side. He was holding a Danish in one hand a styrofoam cup in the other. As he approached one of the uniformed officers the young man stiffened to attention recognizing him immediately.

"Hi Inspector. Coffee's waiting for you over there." He pointed to the old cinder block building that stood off the street about one-hundred and fifty yards away. The tall man grunted in acknowledgement. His angular face was taut, intense, as if his features had been chiseled out of stone. He walked through the gate of the chain link fence and headed in the direction of the officer's pointed finger. Through the open overhead door Bobby Cash could see Captain

Joe Marino, better known as Coffee, talking to two of the homicide lab boys. He was given his nickname years ago when he was walking a beat. At that time he was trying to give up smoking so he carried coffee flavored hard candy in his pocket and sucked on them continually to stop the urge of lighting up a cigarette. Even after he quit he continued the habit of sucking on the dark brown clumps. Anyone standing close to him would get a whiff of the constant coffee fragrance that lingered on his breath.

Out of the corner of his eye Coffee caught a glimpse of the tall figure coming through the dimly lit doorway. There was no mistaking the hulking figure or the determined surefooted gate of the man's stride. Coffee knew Bobby Cash had finally arrived. He barked another order at the lab boys and briskly walked in Bobby's direction.

"For Christ's sake what took you so long? I've been here for over an hour."

Cash's blue eyes squinted and the muscles in his firm jaw flexed as he shot an instant look of disgust at Coffee's prying remark. He ignored the question and asked, "What do you have?"

Coffee, who was well into his sixties, was grossly overweight for his small frame. He had an addiction for pasta and cheap Chianti. He tilted his balding head back and looked up at Bobby.

"That guy over there," he nodded his head at the man sitting on the upside down five gallon bucket, "his name is George Harwood. He was jogging down the street this morning. He came to the intersection out front and waited to cross. A van came along and splashed him with what he thought was a huge puddle of water. Turns out it wasn't water at all. It was a stagnant pool of blood and bits of flesh. One of the locals called in a report when they heard him screaming. The patrol car that was summoned to the scene found him and the source of the blood. That's when we got the call." He hesitated. "It seems this place was once a meat packing house. I guess the electricity went out with the storm and all the meat hanging in the lockers thawed out. Only turns out it ain't the blood from some quartered up cows." He moved closer to Bobby, almost whispering the next few sentences.

"Turns out it's women. Lots of women. All butchered up and hanging on meat hooks. We've got a real psycho here." Coffee's bushy white brows deepened with concern.

"How many?" Bobby calmly asked, as he finished the remainder of his Danish washing it down with the last of his coffee and then he pitched the empty styrofoam cup on the already littered warehouse floor.

"Well, we're not sure. But we've counted five heads, all Caucasian, so there's probably five bodies to match. It's going to be a real jigsaw puzzle putting these women back together. The coroner's going to go crazy!"

"It won't be the first time." Bobby said as he walked away from Coffee and headed towards the meat lockers. Flashes of light could be seen coming from the inside of them. He knew that was the one that held the bodies. The coroner's people were still taking pictures. Outside the locker he saw Dave Johnson dusting for prints.

"How ya doing Dave?" Bobby said putting his hand on Dave's shoulder.

"Hi inspector." he said as he straightened up, from his bent over position. He shook his head indicating his frustration. "I'll tell you, there are more prints on this thing than a whore on her back at a fraternity party. No telling how many people have been coming in and out of here."

Bobby nodded his head in agreement and said, "Do the best you can Dave," He patted him on the back. "and when you're done here, dust the fence gate, the side door, and the overhead. Could be we might get lucky on one of them. Also see if there are any tire tracks you can get a cast out of. I don't think you'll find any with this rain, but give it a shot anyway."

"Sure thing Inspector. At this rate I probably won't be done before lunch time." He smiled, then added. "But who cares. After seeing this, I don't think I'll have much of an appetite anyway." He curled his lips down in an expression of sickness.

Bobby not wanting to be in the way of the photographer or coroner stood at the locker's entrance and looked around. Even he, a seasoned veteran, wasn't prepared for what he saw. The stainless steel locker was about thirty feet long and twenty feet wide. From the ceiling hung four rows of meat hooks on sliding tracks normally used for holding animal carcasses. Some of the hooks were vacant, but more were not. Legs hung from some, arms and shoulders from others, chest and pelvic sections from the rest. Heads were scattered carelessly around the floor. Blondes, brunettes, and one redhead. In the far corner lay a pile of women clothing. Beside them on the floor lay an axe, a hand saw and a butcher knife. The killer was no skilled surgeon. The body parts hanging from the meat hooks had been hacked apart with no rhyme or reason.

Walt Barber had been Cook County's coroner for almost twenty years. He'd seen lots of bad things. He was used to people's sick and gruesome entertainment. He had even witnessed Richard Speck's handiwork. But this one took the cake. He was kneeling beside one of the heads on the floor when he sensed a presence standing behind him. "Hey

Bobby." He said in his friendly country manner. He glanced up at Bobby but stayed in a kneeling position beside the head he was examining. "This one's going to take me some time."

"What's your guess Walt?" Bobby asked as he knelt down next to Walt and the head, to get a better look. He noticed painfully that in life, she had been a real looker. She had long ash blonde hair and was young enough to be Bobby's daughter. Probably in her early twenties.

"Well, one thing's for sure. They've all got fractured skulls. Our killer must have come up from behind and hit each of them hard with some type of blunt instrument. It could have been the axe, but I doubt it. I don't think the indentations would match. My guess is he still has what he used. Probably keeps whatever he used with him." Bobby took a closer look at the wounds at the back of the head.

"Is that how they died?"

"Can't really say Bobby. Not until I get them on the tables."

"Do you think they were sexually abused?"

"That's another thing I can't answer for sure yet. My guess, however, is yes. The pelvic areas are badly bruised. There's also some evidence of sodomy." He sighed at the brutally involved. "He used those things over there, to take them apart." He pointed in the direction of the axe, hand saw and knife that Bobby had noticed earlier. "Notice how old they are? Maybe they're antiques. I told Dave not to bag them until you got the chance to see him. I just thought they were interesting."

"Anything else you noticed, Walt?"

"Yeah, the red head isn't natural." He chuckled to himself and they both rose to their feet. "As I said Bobby," he got serious again, "this one is going to be tough. We don't know how long they've been here. At these temperatures they could have been frozen for months. It's going to be almost impossible to pinpoint the time and date of their deaths. Also it's going to be a while before we know who goes to who."

Bobby dodged between the hanging body parts and walked over to the pile of clothing. He picked up a blue blouse. It felt like silk. It looked expensive. The label inside the blouse read, "Jones of New York". He dropped it and picked up a red V-neck sweater. It read, "J.C. Penny". One didn't seem to go with the other. He stood back up.

"Just do your best Walt. Call me when you get anything." He looked Walt straight in the eye. "And I mean anything!" Walt understood the repercussions that came from this type of homicide. The police liked to solve them as quickly as possible to keep the public from panicking and the press from having a field day. He signaled Bobby with his hand and finger pointed like a cocked gun. He understood what he meant. Bobby continued. "You can pack them up when you're ready. Oh, and Walt, don't give out any information to the press just yet." Walt knew what he was going to say before he even said it.

"You got it Bobby. See you at the morgue." He turned his back and went back to his grim work.

Bobby walked back to where Coffee was standing next to a shivering George Hardwood. Someone had given him a regulation starchy gray blanket to cover his blood soaked body.

"Can I go home now, Captain? I've told you everything I know." He looked pale and vulnerable from his experience.

"Hey Winters!" Coffee yelled at the young rookie leaning against the office door just inside the overhead. "Make yourself useful and give Mr. Harwood here a lift home." The rookie's temporary pallid colored complexion seemed to brighten at the opportunity to leave the scene of his first homicide.

"Useless as tits on a nun." Coffee chuckled.

Bobby's semblance of a smile was more of a jeer than a grin. Coffee didn't seem to notice and he couldn't contain the belly laugh that came from his own joke.

"These kids today! They just don't seem to have what it takes anymore. No balls!" Coffee spit out between snorts of laughter.

Bobby's mind wandered back to the first grisly murder scene he had witnessed. A young woman had been bludgeoned to death by her lover. Her body lay on the floor of her bedroom in a pool of blood. Her face looked like hamburger meat as did much of the rest of her. Blood had been splattered everywhere. Calmly sitting on a chair next to her dressing table sat the coroner. A spilled box of Godiva chocolates lay on the floor next to him. Just as Bobby walked into the room, the coroner picked up a piece of the delectable chocolate. He wiped off the fresh drops of blood that clung like cherry syrup to the sweet milk chocolate coating on the outside, and popped it into his mouth. Bobby barely made it out of the room before he lost his dinner and most of his lunch on the living room floor. He was embarrassed by his actions and flushed a bright crimson as the older cops teased him about his rookie reaction. Now however, he could eat all the chocolate like that if he wanted to. It didn't bother him anymore. He was used to violence an it's consequences. Then the sound of Coffee's voice brought him back to reality and the present.

"Bobby, the only thing we figure, is this guy must have had a key to this place. There isn't a window or door lock broken anywhere and the women's belongings are as naked as they are. Not a clue to their identification. We'll print them and hope we get lucky."

"Call me when you get an I.D. on any of them Coffee. And let me know if your dicks turn up anything from beating the bushes." He turned away from Coffee and walked out of the dimly-lit warehouse and back into the bright, mid-morning sun. It was going to be a long day.

CHAPTER 3

Kodak stood inside the main gate just behind the police barricade. He had been Bobby Cash's partner for a little more than two and a half years. As a matter of fact, Bobby was the one responsible for him becoming a cop.

He had grown up in the ghetto where his mama had taken in laundry and cleaned floors to support the family. He had never known his father and, for that matter, didn't want to. One sunny June afternoon his mama sent him to the Cake Box Bakery to buy day old bread and rolls. The bakery was located four blocks from his house, right across the street from Wilson's Liquor Store. As he was coming out of the bakery he'd heard gunshots, a not too uncommon sound in his neighborhood. Two young punks, both black, had come running out of Wilson's Liquor Store and had crossed over to his side of the street about seventy-five feet in front of him. They had both looked at Kodak as they ran past him. That was their first mistake.

Within fifteen minutes two squad cars pulled up in front of Wilson's Liquor Store. Kodak joined the crowd of gawkers who were peeking in the front door of the liquor store. Old man Wilson had been shot three times, once in the head and twice in the chest. His wife of forty years, lay four feet from him in a pool of her own blood. Her throat had been slit, ear to ear.

As the cops moved the crowd of people aside to rope off the area two other cars pulled up. The side door of the first car was marked, Cook County M. E. The other car was plain black with no markings. Kodak could still remember how the large man in the unmarked card seemed to uncoil as he got out and walked inside the liquor store where the cops had already begun their investigation. That had been Kodak's first glimpse of Bobby Cash.

Kodak stood, mingling in with the crowd, as two uniformed cops walked among them and asked for information any of them might have picked up on the killers. One of the cops finally made his way over to Kodak and asked, "Did you see anything?" Kodak responded with a detailed description of the two men he saw running away from the scene of the crime.

"You'd better come with me." The young cop said as he guided Kodak inside the liquor store to introduce him to Captain Anderson. "Captain Anderson, this here is Thomas Webster. He got a real good luck at our suspects."

"Thanks Tolls." Coffee said. The young cop turned knowing by Coffee's tone that he had been dismissed. He headed back out to the street to continue questioning the crowd.

"Well have a seat over here Thomas and tell me exactly what you saw." Coffee pointed to the Seagram 7 case that was sitting on the floor.

Kodak walked over and sat down. Bobby who had been leaning against the wall displaying the bourbons and listened as Thomas proceeded to describe the two men to Coffee. When he was finished Bobby skeptically asked him how he could be so sure of what the two men looked like since they had both been running at break neck speed at least seventy-five yards in front of him. Kodak turned to him, smiled, and gave him an example.

"Old man Wilson has on a red plaid shirt, gray pants, and brown shoes and socks. He has a birth mark that is shaped like a maple leaf on the back of his left hand, along with s slim gold wedding band. Mrs. Wilson is wearing a lime green dress, white sweater, brown nylons and white shoes. She also has on a gold wedding band, only hers is wider.

Coffee and Bobby looked at each other in amazement. The bodies lay twenty-five feet behind them, on the other side of the counter and cash register.

"I have what they call total recall." Kodak explained. "When I see something my mind kind of takes a picture and stores it in my brain."

"Well Kodak, let's go downtown and look through some mug books. I want to see just how good that camera in your head works." That was the first time Bobby or anyone had called him Kodak. Now the whole force knew him by that name.

Bobby took him downtown where he identified the two killers. Bobby also helped him finish his education and enter the police academy. His mama didn't have to take in laundry or scrub floors for a living after that and he owed it all to Bobby.

Now he was doing what he did best. He stood there, his arms folded across his chest, feet slightly apart, watching the crowd and cars passing in front of him. It never ceased to amaze Kodak the number of murderers who would turn up in the crowd of spectators just to watch all the excitement they had created. He nailed many of them when all the clues were finally put together.

As he watched the crowd, a dark blue pick-up with high wooden sides approached. It moved slowly in the line of traffic. A traffic cop who was blowing his whistle and waving his hands, was trying to lend order to the confusion. The man in the pick-up looked over at the warehouse where all the commotion was coming from. His cold black eyes took in everything including the black man with the mirrored sunglasses who was standing just inside the gate. He also noticed the large man standing just in front of the overhead door. For a moment, their eyes seemed to meet. The driver's hand was holding tightly onto his bearded chin. His elbow was resting on the window frame since his window was rolled down. A large, (fouled) anchor was tattooed on his bare upper arm. He was staring so hard he didn't even notice the traffic cop blowing his whistle at him. The cop startled him when he walked up to the side of his truck and yelled, "Ya got a problem buddy? Move it!" The bearded man stepped on the gas and slowly drove down the street and out of sight.

Even Kodak with his total recall could not have seen into the back of the pick-up truck as it drove pass him. For if he had, he would have seen a large, green canvas bag laying on the floor. It was squirming slightly. It contained victim number six.

CHAPTER 4

Bobby slowly inched his unmarked car through the huge crowd of gawkers that had gathered around the meat packing plant. They were standing on their toes and craning their necks in order to get a better look at all the blood and horror that goes with murder. When he finally got past the crowd and reached the clear pavement he glanced in his rear view mirror. He could still see Kodak, standing like the Klacto robot in the movie, 'The Day the Earth Stood Still'. He looked as if he were keeping vigil on all the unknown earthlings that surrounded him. Only his head and eyes moved. Bobby smiled to himself as he recalled the first time the two of them had met.

He proceeded onto the Kennedy express way and headed towards downtown Chicago. In the twenty minutes it took him to drive to headquarters he barely noticed the traffic that sped pass him on the expressway, his thoughts were on the killer of the five women. His gut instinct told him that if an act of God had not shut off the power in the cooler, the body count in the meat locker would have continued to climb.

The head of one of the young girls flashed before his eyes. He knew that somewhere someone was missing her, wanting her back. But she was never coming back. None of them were.

As if the car guided itself, he realized that he had come to a stop. His car was already in its assigned parking space. The small, white sign in front of him read 'B. Cash'.

He entered the station house through the main doors, walked pass the officer at the front desk and proceeded up the flight of stairs that would take him to the Homicide Department. Behind him he heard the familiar mixture of noises that come from victims and criminals alike. Soft sobbing, screaming and shouting all blended together in a sort of abstract symphony. You heard what you wanted to hear, tuned out what you didn't.

When he opened the door to the Homicide Department the symphony instantly changed and he was greeted, instead by the muddling of voices intertwined with the sound of typewriters being used to pound out reports. Station 101 WLAK played 'Oldies but Goodies' softly in the background.

No one seemed to acknowledge his presence when he walked through the door except Detective Mike Hardy who was talking loudly on the phone then nodding his head in agreement to whomever was on the other end of the line. He raised his free arm to wave to Bobby when he saw him enter the room. Bobby waved back and walked over to the coffee machine. The detectives referred to it as 'the machine that never rested' He poured a cup of the strong, bitter brew and walked back into the maze of desks that occupied half of the entire second floor. The other detectives, now aware of his presence, greeted him with a nod or 'Good Morning', as he made his way to the private, glass-enclosed office he occupied at the back of the building.

He closed the door behind him and sat down at his old desk. He was sure it was older than he was. He swung his chair around and propped his feet up on the window sill. He leaned back and stared at the office building across the street. In the quiet of his office his mind returned once more to the morning's events. He wondered about the kind of mind who could mutilated a woman that way, and what it was that made him capable of such violence. Serial killers were becoming more common in today's world. Most however, killed and possibly raped their victims without mutilating their body. A great percentage of killings were crimes of passion, such as the dentist in Texas, who had cut his wife apart with a chain saw. The guy claimed he did it because he didn't want to pay her alimony. Ex-husbands from all over the country had sent him letters and telegrams saying 'well done'. Multiple mutilations such as the victims they had found this morning were uncommon. Jack the Ripper was probably one of the world's most infamous serial killers and he had never been caught, at least not legally. Bobby made a mental note to stop in and see Patti Jacobs the department's criminal psychologist. She would probably be able to give him a pretty good profile on this 'Jack'.

The phone rang interrupting Bobby's thoughts. He wheeled around on his chair to answer it. "Ya".

"Inspector Cash, this is Officer Tom Harper, burglary. Lieutenant McKibbe wants you down here, on the double. He's got something important for you in the Davis case".

"Tell him I'm on my way." Bobby hung up the phone. So much for his peace and quiet he thought as he gulped down what was left of his coffee.

Burglary was on the lower floor, behind general complaints and misdemeanors. Rather than entering from the front of the building as he had earlier, he took the back stairwell which came out by the interrogation rooms. As he walked into burglary he spotted Danny McKibben sitting on a desk talking to another officer. He didn't recognize the other officer. Danny stood up and held out his hand when he saw Bobby approach.

"Hi Bobby". He said as they firmly shook hands. "I have something for you. I think this is going really going to make your day."

"Well at the rate it's going anything would be an improvement."

Danny turned to the unidentified officer and said, "Bobby this is Officer Dave Martin. Officer Martin this is the infamous Inspector Bobby Cash." Bobby shook hands with Officer Martin.

"Officer Martin comes to us courtesy of Precinct #12. You know, over by the Park Ridge area." Danny continued, "Officer Martin why don't you tell Inspector Cash what happened."

"Well, Inspector, for the last two weeks we've had this stake out set up on a house over at 2135 Beacon Lane. The house had been vacant for almost six months when the owner rented it to what he described as a nice young couple by the name of Mr. and Mrs. John Wright. Anyway there's this woman who lives next door to this house, a Mrs. Ethel Morris. She's they neighborhood busybody. She tries to be friendly with this couple but they won't give her the time of day so she gets her nose bent out of joint. Well, she sees these vans pulling in and out at all times of the night and day, with men carrying all kinds of electronics and appliances in and out of the place. She has this key to the place since she used to check on it for the previous owners when they were out of town. Anyways, one day when she's sure they're gone, she goes over and goes inside. The Wrights had never changed the locks. Big mistake. Well, if you know the area, Inspector, the houses there are big four and five bedrooms with all the trimmings. Mrs. Morris goes inside and finds TVs, stereos, silver and the like all over the place. So she rushes home and tips us off. We go and check out Mr. and Mrs. Wright. He's an insurance agent for a local company and she sells cosmetics at Lord and Taylor over in North Court. He's driving a new Porsche and she a new BMW. We check out they're finances and find out they're only knocking down thirty eight thousand dollars a year between the both of them."

Bobby was getting impatient. "I've got your general drift Officer Martin. But was does this have to do with me and the Davis case?"

As if reading his mind Officer Martin replied, "if you'll be patient just a little longer, I'm getting to the point."

Bobby shifted his weight to his other foot.

"So we start staking out the place. We hit it this morning while two guys are unloading a van. We picked up both of them and Mrs. Wright. The house was stacked full of hot items. The only uncluttered place in the house was the bedroom and I'm walking through it when I see this jewelry box on the dresser. I picked it up and Mrs. Wright screams, 'that's mine'. I took it anyway. The hot list is checked against her jewelry and guess what?"

He reached behind him and brought out a small plastic evidence bag. Inside was a pair of emerald and diamond earrings and five carat emerald and diamond ring.

Bobby gently took the bag out of his hand and said, "Lynn Davis?"

Officer Martin smiled like the Cheshire Cat. "That's right Inspector! The two goons said they had nothing to do with it. According to them John Wright had to have pulled the trigger. They claimed they weren't even there. And the wife, she ain't talking."

Bobby wasn't totally listening to what Officer Martin was saying anymore. He was recalling that day almost two months ago when they had found the body of Lynn Davis. She had been a successful real estate agent. The day of her murder she spent the entire day at an open house in Wilmett. Her son was supposed to pick her up at 5:00 P.M. to take her to dinner. When he arrived he found the door to the house wide open. He walked in calling her name but got no answer. He finally found her in down stairs powder room. She had been shot twice in the back. Apparently the killer told her to give him the diamond and emerald ring that was on her finger. When she couldn't get it off, she had evidently walked over to the sink to put soap and water on her hands to help. The killer must have grown impatient and shot her in the back and cut off her finger to get the ring. There were no fingerprints and no witnesses.

Danny's voice broke in, "We've got an A.P.B. out on Wright. He didn't know about the heat this morning so he's probably hanging around just like any 'Joe Citizen'. I'll call you as soon as he's in custody if he isn't already. We've got his wife in holding. You want to talk to her?"

Bobby wasn't prepare for what he saw when he walked through the door of the interrogation door. Sandy Wright was lovely. She looked like she just had stepped off the cover of Vogue rather than out of a jail cell. In the thirty minutes he was with her she never uttered a word, not even when he told her she would be accused as an accessory to murder. Her huge blue eyes opened slightly wider but that was the only reaction he got. He finally left her.

He suddenly felt older than his forty-seven years. He knew his feelings had been triggered by Sandy Wright. By the time she got out of prison she would be much older than what he was now. What a waste!

He glanced at his watch and noticed that it was already 12:20 P.M. Instead of going back to his office he decided to drive over to administration to see if he could round up Patti Jacobs. He knew he should call her first to set up an appointment but he didn't really feel like going back to his office. Besides, he thought to himself, the drive will do him good.

Administration was located near the corner of Dearborn and Madison, the site of Chicago's first School House. Bobby pulled his car into the west parking lot marked 'Personnel'. He looked over at the building. It was surrounded by four huge granite pillars that resembled some ancient Roman temple. Inside the floors and walls had all been finished in sand colored marble. His foot steps echoed behind him as he crossed the lobby and headed towards the main bank of elevators that were located on the ground floor. Once in the elevator he pushed the button to take him to the third floor. He got off and walked down the long hallway past a series of government offices until he reached the office at the end of the hall. The sign on the door read:

Patricia Jacobs

Criminal Physiologist, B. Ph.

Bobby opened the door to find the reception area empty. He walked over to Patti's office since the door was already slightly ajar. "Patti?" he called out as he pushed the door the rest of the way open.

A middle aged woman with short curly gray hair, jumped back from Patti's desk, knocking over a stack of files in the process.

"Young man, what are you doing here? You scared me to death!" She exclaimed as she bent down to gather the scattered papers.

"I'm sorry Ma'am. I was looking for Patti Jacobs. Can you tell me where can I find her?"

"I certainly can, but I certainly won't! She'll be back around 3:00 P.M. come back then."

Bobby removed his badge and identification from his back pocket. He held them out in front of him. "I'm Inspector Cash ma'am. I'm here on Police business now, where is she?"

Mario's Restaurant was located in the basement of the R & J Office Building on Dearborn Street. It took Bobby's eyes a few seconds to adjust to the dimly lit interior but once his eyes adjusted he liked what he saw. Tables were scattered about the room, each draped with the familiar red and white checkered table cloth. Small Tiffany lights hung above each table and empty Chanti bottles were being used for candles holders. All were lit. The bar was located on the right hand side of the room. Small lights were intertwined with the wooden lattice work at the bar and twinkled in the dark room to fill it with a soft romantic atmosphere.

As Bobby eyes adjusted to the dark room he searched for Patti. He spotted her sitting alone at a back corner table with a drink in one hand and a book in the other. Patti wasn't easy to miss. Her long, frosted blonde hair hung almost to the middle of her back. He couldn't see her cat colored green eyes or those large sensuous lips, that were hidden behind the book she was reading, but he didn't have to see them. He knew they were there. At one time the two of them had shared more than just criminal information. He sat down in one of the empty chairs beside her. She put her book down and looked up at him.

"I've been expecting you." A a waiter appeared at their table with another vodka martini for her and a scotch on the rocks for him. When the waiter turned and left Patti looked over at Bobby and smiled smugly.

"I guess you have." He raised his glass to her and took a deep swallow. "You must have heard about this morning."

"Everybody has. It's the talk of the whole department." She stirred her drink with one of her long manicured fingertips. "I've been working on your killer's profile. I knew sooner or later you'd be knocking on my door. That's why I gave the waiter instructions to bring you a double Grant's on the rocks when you showed up. I knew you were going to need it."

As he looked into her eyes he could still remember the long warm winter nights they had shared just last year.

"So what did you find out about our 'Jack the Ripper'? What do you think makes him tick?"

"Well without having any psychological background information on him, I can only go with histories of similar serial killers, try to combined them, an come up with anything they all have in common. One common thread the all seem to have, is they are all either temporarily or permanently psychotic."

Bobby gave her a look that seemed to say, come on and tell me something I don't already know.

Ignoring his look, she continued. "Most of them I've read about hate a woman somewhere, either a mother, lover or wife. They've usually had a long history of emotional disturbances. They tend to commit the murder, or murderers, right after a period of intense mental stress. Your killer is probably anti-social, a loner, and perhaps even an alcoholic. Many of these people suffer front poor self-esteem. They usually have poor work records. Butchering the women and hanging them on meat hooks maybe symbolic for him. He probably enjoys it. There could be endless contributing factors, but the ones I've just mentioned are generally the most common. One thing I know for sure Bobby. He won't stop. He won't stop until you catch him!"

CHAPTER 5

The sounds of sirens helped Ellen Parker regain partial consciousness. She couldn't see anything in the blackness that surrounded her. The heavy adhesive tape that covered her mouth prevented her groans of pain from being heard. Blood oozed from the wound in the back of her head. Her body bounced slightly with the movements beneath her. Her arms and legs were bound with the same heavy tape that kept her movements to a minimum. She couldn't quite remember where she was or how she got there. She only knew that she was tired, so very tired, and very cold. The last image she recalled before lapsing back into unconsciousness was of her sister Ann's face, her bright shining face. She could still see those mischievous light brown eyes that fit her effervescent personality so perfectly. Ellen, on the other hand, had always been called the dark and serious one. No one had ever accused the two of them of looking like sisters, at least not until they saw them with their parents.

Their father was German with a fair complexion, like Ann, while their mother, who was of Greek descent, possessed the same jet black hair and olive complexion as Ellen. What a handsome couple they made. Ellen could still remember how proud she had been of her parents when she was a child in school. At the parent-teacher functions her girlfriends would giggled and whisper about how beautiful her mother was.

Ann and Ellen had always been close. They spent most of their young impressionable years growing up on a farm in the Northwestern part of Illinois. Farms there, like playmates, were few and far between. Most of the time they only had each other. Their father raised cattle and hogs and their mother hated it. Ellen could remember her mother's expression the day the pharmaceutical company offered to buy them out. She was overjoyed at the prospect of finally getting off the farm and moving back to civilization. Several months after the offer they had packed up everything and moved into a three bedroom ranch style house in the Chicago suburb of Arlington Heights. Her mother was delighted to finally be in a house with, as she would say, all the modern conveniences.

Even though she and Ann made their new friends in different circles, they had remained as close as ever. Now they were both married and lived in the suburbs but almost thirty miles apart. Never the less, barring the distance and their hectic schedules they still found time to get together for lunch and girl talk every couple of weeks.

As Ellen lapsed back into semi-consciousness she recalled the last visit with her sister. She could see Ann's mouth moving a mile a minute with her usual enthusiasm. But there was no sound to Ellen's vision. Then, as if somebody had turned up the volume of a television, Ellen began to relive their conversation of just a few days before.

"Ellie, I can't wait till you see it. It's not big, mind you, only two bedrooms. But the living room has the biggest stone fireplace you've ever seen. Every room in the house has a beautiful view of either the lake or the woods."

Ellen smiled watching her sister bubble over with happiness.

Her sister stopped to catch her breath and continued, "and Tom, he's so excited. He'll finally be able to get that sail boat he's always wanted. He said he's going to start looking for one the moment we move in. I know that Lake Geneva is more than sixty miles from you Ellie but you, Adam, and Amy can come spend weekends with us anytime you want. We'll go sailing and hiking. We'll have a wonderful time! You just wait and see."

Then as if someone was once again adjusting the volume dials on the television the picture began to fade and Ann disappeared into the blackness. Then again the television was turning back on. This time she was driving somewhere in the city when she saw it, the sail boat weather vane. It was beautiful. What a perfect house warming present for Ann and Tom. They would love it. She could picture it perched high up in their new cottage in the woods and the sun's rays glistening off of the cooper colored metal. She had to get it for them. She must. She reached for it but it kept moving further and further away from her. Then she saw that Adam had it. Adam was keeping it from her. Adam her husband, the man she had loved for so many years, the father of their little girl Amy—dear, sweet Amy.

Her mind tumbled back in time, to the first time she and Adam had made love. They spent the day up in Wisconsin skiing Alpine Valley. One thing led to another and Adam had finally ended up getting a room for the two of them at the lodge. She remembered how she stood, blushing at his side, sure that the hotel desk clerk knew they were not really Mr. and Mrs. Adam Jameson. She was not a virgin but Adam had shown her the difference between love and sex that night.

The room they shared was warm. A soft orange glow emanated from the fire that crackled in the fireplace. Room service brought up a chilled bottle of Chardonnay with two glasses. Together they lay, side by side, on the floor before the fire. Their bodies reach out to each other. They kissed. Touched. Adam lovingly removed her ski sweater and began suckling gently on her breast. Her whole body begged for further pleasures. He ever so gently removed her jeans and panties, never interrupting those gentle kisses. He stood in front of the dancing shadows from the fire to remove his clothes. He knelt down beside her. Her skin quivered at his touch. Gently he eased apart her legs. His lips and tongue explored the heart of her femininity ever so slowly at first, then faster and faster until biting the back of her own hand was the only way to contain the screams of pleasure that came from the first orgasm she had ever experienced.

Adam was always so very gentle, so patient. But know he was hurting her. He was biting her nipples. His nails dug deep into her flesh as he pushed his hardness deep into her groin. He pushed harder and harder. Bruising her. Hurting her. Then, treating her as if she was some sort of animal, he grabbed her and rolled her over onto her stomach. He spread her legs wide and pried apart her buttocks with his fingers.

"No Adam! No!"

He had never done this to her before.

"Stop Adam! Please stop!"

She started to scream but the tape over her mouth kept the screams from coming out in her partial consciousness. The dreams left her. Reality returned. She realized that it wasn't Adam who was doing these horrible things to her. It was the stranger, the sail boat man.

"God help me. Please help me!" She silently begged. As the pains ripped through her body she returned to the welcome blackness where she once again felt no pain.

As her limbs were being severed from her body her last thoughts were of Adam and Amy. "Oh God, what will they do without me?"

CHAPTER 6

A long leisurely lunch was a luxury that Bobby seldom afforded himself, but between Mario, Patti and the promise of fresh Mussels in garlic butter and perfectly prepared Veal Piccata the temptation was too great. Bobby succumbed to a first real unrushed meal he'd had in a long time.

By the time he finished his meal and returned to his car he was not at all surprised when dispatch informed him that Walt wanted him at the morgue. Walt was one of the country's most respected pathologist and Bobby knew he would waste no time literally in this case putting the pieces back together.

As he approached the entrance of the morgue he recognized several cars that belonged to the media parked out front. Since he wasn't ready to deal with questions he couldn't answer yet he pulled around to the back entrance and parked next to one of the several hearses that belonged to the city.

The morgue occupied and old red, brick building that had been built around the turn of the century. The city had planned to tear it down and build a modern facility in its place but the historical society had argued about the morgue's historical significance since many of the world's most famous and notorious gangsters bullet riddled bodies rested there. The historical society eventually won the battle and the façade of the structure had been restored to its original beauty, if one could truly call a morgue beautiful. The city, not wanting to be upstaged, completely renovated the entire interior of the building. From the outside on-lookers had no indication that the most modern forensic medical equipment was contained inside.

Bobby could smell the strong formaldide as soon as the automatic doors silently slid open admitting him into this building designed exclusively for the dead. He walked past glass enclosed offices and labs, each bursting with activity, as he made his way to the large stainless-steel, tiled dissecting room. As he entered the room he spotted Walt who was totally absorbed in his work, and just about to make his first incision in the limbless torso of one of the five dead women.

Bobby had seen Walt performed so many autopsies he felt sure that he could perform the procedure blindfolded himself. First the heavy scalpel blade moved quickly from the left shoulder cutting straight across the chest. Next the customary 'V' was cut so that it opened the victim's chest. Another incision traveled from the midline of the abdomen, missing the navel, to just above the pubic hairline. The skin, at the point of the 'V', would be pulled back and a number of cuts would be made through the muscle and fat through the clavicle and breastbone. Only a Stryker saw was needed to open the rib cage and exposed the internal organs that lay beneath.

Bobby listened while Walt talked into the pedal controlled microphone that hung above the stainless-steel table. He described the technique, step by step, recording every detail of his work. His report would be kept on file at the Medical Examiner's Office. He stopped the procedure at the point when the Styker saw would have been necessary, took his foot off the pedal and motioned for Bobby to join him.

"Bobby, as you well know, I normally wouldn't call you down here until I've autopsied all five of your victims. However, since they were all in pieces I decided to autopsy the heads first, mainly because they all suffered similar traumas to the skull. I wanted to know if the traumas suffered were severe enough to be the one common denominator responsible for their deaths."

Walt walked away from the partially opened torso and over to the refrigerated coolers that lined one wall of the room. Each cooler was large enough to hold four bodies, stacked one upon the other, on the adjustable sliding metal tables. The table that Walt slid out contained the five heads Bobby had seen earlier that morning. Walt looked over each head as if he were trying to choose the perfect cantaloupe at the supermarket. He found two heads that satisfied him, put one under each arm and walked over to an empty bisecting table.

Bobby thought Walt, his hands and apron front were covered in blood looked almost comical, in a ghoulish sort of way, as he lugged the two heads across the room. Walt carefully laid each head face down on the table. Then with one expert motion he pulled back the scalp, which was almost completely severed from the skull, to expose the naked bone from head up.

"Look here Bobby." He pointed to the section at the back of the skull that had been damaged by the killer's weapon.

Bobby bent down to get a closer look.

"Hemorrhaging was moderately heavy, but here's the interesting thing", Walt said as he suddenly twisted his hand to remove the entire top of the skull. His motion left the brain exposed for full view. "See here. The brain has suffered no significant trauma, only slight swelling and bruising."

"You mean the blow to her didn't kill her?"

"No Bobby and not only that. Look over here on her right side." He turned the head slightly so Bobby could get a better view. "Notice the dark mass? The blood congealed there at its lowest level. That means she died with her head on."

"So you mean they were all dead before they were hacked apart?"

"Not exactly. Come over here."

They walked back to the unfinished corpse. Wait picked up the Stryker saw and continued where he left off cutting quickly through the ribs. The organs lay exposed, like the clear plastic inserts in an anatomy 1 textbook. Walt gently pushed them aside.

"Notice the small amount of congealed blood? The body is almost devoid of fluid. That means the heart continued to pump blood through the disconnected arteries. The others I've already examined are the same and I'm willing to bet the rest are too. The cause of death was bleeding. They each bleed to death!"

"Jesus Walt!" Bobby exclaimed. "What are you telling me? Did guy deliberately know what he is doing? Did he cut these women to pieces knowing they were still alive?"

"It can't be coincidence. No one could fuck up five murders. He hit them hard enough just to maim them, not kill them."

Bobby shook his head. The thought was too terrible to imagine.

"Now, let's get back to the weapon he used." Walt walked over to his instrument table, picked up a magnifying glass, and returned to the dissecting table where the two heads lay.

Bobby followed him. Walt held the magnifying glass just above the wound at the base of the skull. "What do you see?"

Bobby looked into it. "Well, it looks like the surface surrounding the wound is ruptured in a sort of grid pattern, kind of like the pattern of a waffle iron."

"Exactly. Now what kind of a weapon makes that kind of impression? In all my years, I've never seen anything like it. And look here." Walt took a pair of tweezers and pulled a minute splinter from the inside of the wound. Holding it up in front of Bobby he said, "and whatever it is, it's made of wood. The lab is trying to identify the species of wood."

"Wonderful!" Bobby said sarcastically. "I've got a killer loose who gets some type of sadistic pleasure out of hacking off the arms and legs of live women. He's been out there, undetected, for God only knows how long and he's using a weapon that Forensic can't identify. Next you'll probably tell me they were all raped and sodomized too."

The look in Walt's eyes revealed the truth that lay behind Bobby's last remark. All Walt could say was "Bingo."

"Oh no! Bobby moaned.

"Oh no what?" Coffee said as he cracked open the door to the dissecting room.

"Oh, nothing." said Bobby. "Doc here, was just telling me that our killer makes 'Ivan the Terrible' look like Mr. Rogers and he's fucking up our neighborhood!"

"Now, now." said Coffee. "I know this day hasn't exactly been going your way especially since burglary got the collar on the Davis case but let's not blow things out of perspective." He chuckled to himself seeing, from the look on Bobby's face that the part on the Davis case struck a nerve.

"Walt, why don't you give Coffee here a lesson in perspective and knock that shit-eating grin off his face?"

Bobby could remember the last time Coffee told him he was blowing things out of perspective. It had been about six years ago, a year before he made Inspector. A call came over the radio requesting a car to respond to a complaint in the Norridge area. A woman there had called in a complaint saying there were screams coming from her next door neighbor's house. A patrol car in the vicinity had picked up the call and responded. Bobby had decided to tag along, just in case they needed backup since his position was almost as close to the scene as the responding car.

The Norridge area was an old, well kept section on the north side of Chicago. A huge Catholic church and school served as its hub, making it a prime location for young, mostly Irish and Polish families to raise their children. Most of the homes in the area were identical three bedroom bungalows which stood on postage stamp sized lots. Garages were located at the rear of the property. The builder in the area had lacked imagination except when it came to the front porches which varied in size, roof design, materials and color. The people who lived in this neighborhood felt relatively safe and secure since the major crime index for the area was well below the nationally reported average.

As Bobby pulled his car up behind the squad car that had taken the call, he could see the two officers standing on a well lit porch. They were talking with the woman who had turned in the complaint. After she finished telling them what had happened, they left her and walked across the lawn to the house next door where the reported screams came from.

The house was dark and silent except for a small light coming form one of the back rooms. Because of the reputation of the neighborhood, the two officers were probably not as alarmed as they should approaching the front door.

"Mr. Pololski, this is the police. Open up!" one of the officers yelled as he banged on the front door. When he received no response, he repeated the action. The front porch light turned on and the two officers relaxed waiting for Mr. Pololski to open the door. Bobby reached for the ignition keys preparing to leave. He assumed, as he was sure the two officers did, they were dealing with just another domestic squabble.

The shot gun blast that rang out through the clear, crisp, autumn air immediately turned peace into pandemonium and life into death. The blast knocked Officer Raymond Cabot clean off the porch. He was now laying on his back, half on and half off the bottom stairs with a gaping hole in his chest. Bobby immediately called dispatch to request back-up and an ambulance for the downed officer. He got out of his car on the street side and ran up the grass between the two houses in order to reach the front porch where the trapped officer was lying.

"Officer Cabot, are you all right? I'm Detective Cash." Dispatch had given him the names of the two officers at the scene.

"Yea, I'm fine. But I'm not Cabot. Cabot's down. I'm Dickerson."

"Stay where you are." Bobby said in little more than a whisper. "Back-up is on the way. Don't let him get out of the front door. I'm going around back to see if I can find a way in."

Quickly and silently, Bobby made his way to the back of the house. A concrete step led up to the back door. The windows were too high for Bobby to look through, much less climb through, and the back door offered no protection so he crept back to the side of the house where he had seen two basement windows. The first one he tried to open was locked, but the second one wasn't. He pushed the window open and entered feet first hoping the wall space beneath him was clear of any unseen obstacles or breakable objects. Luckily it was. As his feet touched the basement floor he thought being tall definitely had its advantages.

The room was pitch black. Bobby reached into his jacket pocket and pulled out a cigarette lighter. He was in the habit of carrying it although he had almost completely quit smoking. The flame from the lighter illuminated the room. "Who said smoking is not a good for your health." he muttered to himself. He was glad he still carried the lighter and was pleased with the light it offered.

The wooden stairs creaked slightly beneath his weight as he made his way towards the top of the stairs. He assumed the stairs came out in the kitchen or hallway as they did in most older homes. As he approached the top of the stairs he wondered how he would get through the door undetected. If the door was unlocked it wouldn't pose a problem. Then the sound of the sirens reached his ears and offered just the distraction he needed.

The door offered no resistance and made little noise as he pushed it open to find himself standing in the dimly lit kitchen. As his eyes were adjusting to the low light he heard a low groan. Lying on the floor between the stove and the kitchen table he could just make out the body of a woman. He carefully made his way through the broken dishes and the overturned chairs to reach Mr. Pololski. Small streams of blood trickled out of the four knife wounds in her chest. Her breathing was shallow and labored.

Bobby heard Coffee over the louder speaker. He was trying to get Mr. Pololski to surrender and throw out his weapon. The street in front of the house had come alive with lights and people.

As quickly and quietly as possible, Bobby made his way to the entrance of the living room. He stole a glance from behind the door jam and saw that Mr. Pololski was kneeling on the couch. His back faced Bobby. He had positioned himself so that he could keep vigil through the side of the front window drapes. The shotgun was at his side and ready to fire. He did not hear Bobby sneak up behind him. But he did feel the cold muzzle of Bobby's 38 against the back of his head.

"Drop it!"

Samuel Pololski heard the click of the cocked revolver. The confrontation was over. Mr. Pololski was escorted to jail in handcuffs. Mrs. Pololski received four pints of blood and two months of hospital care. Officer Raymond Cabot received the Badge of Honor and the best funeral the police officials of the city of Chicago could give him.

Coffee and Bobby were both involved in helping the court reach a decision on whether or not Samuel Pololski was competent to stand trial. During the assessment of Mr. Pololski, the state psychiatrist, Dr. harry Goldberg, discovered that Mary and Samuel Pololski had been married for twenty-three years. They had two grown children. Both were married. One lived on Pittsburgh,the other in Atlanta. Mary Pololski had asked Samuel for a divorce. When he refused a court order to have him removed from the house. he went crazy, said she'd wrecked his life and had made him the laughing stock of the neighborhood. He said he was going to kill her. During the psychiatric review he told the doctor that the day he got out of prison he was still going to kill her. The psychiatrist said that Mr. Pololski was completely unstable and he believed he would carry out his threat if given the chance.

Coffee had called the whole thing a sham. According to him it was a way for the state to keep the nut out of the gas chamber. Three years later, on the second of November, Coffee received a call from Dr. Goldberg who told him that, even though he had voiced his protest to the Board of Directors, they had decided to release Pololski from the State Mental Institution.

"I do believe," he told Coffee, "that this man is still extremely unstable and it's quite possible he will carry out his threats against Mrs. Pololski."

"You're blowing smoke up your ass, Doc. He wouldn't come within fifty miles of her. He's probably on his way to California or Florida by now. I'm sure your fears are unfounded." Coffee's voice was condescending. "Don't worry Doc. We'll take care of it." He hung up the phone before the Doctor could answer him.

When Bobby arrived at Headquarters, almost two hours later, Coffee couldn't resist the temptation to gloat about the phone call he'd had from, as put it, "that hot shot shrink."

"What did Mrs. Pololski say when you called her?" Bobby asked.

"I didn't call her. There's no sense worrying her over nothing. This guy's all bark and no bite." Coffee said grinning.

"Coffee, you asshole!" Bobby grabbed the phone. "Give me the number of Mrs. Pololski on Nottingham." He waited impatiently until the computerized voice gave him the phone number. He glanced at his watch and quickly dialed the number. It was 4:43 P.M. "No answer!" He slammed the phone down.

"She's probably out shopping or something. I'm telling you, there's nothing to worry about. You're blowing this whole thing out of perspective."

If looks could kill the one Bobby flashed Coffee would have laid him to rest. "Well, I'm going over there." Bobby said through clenched teeth.

"All right. I'll go with you just to show you that you're wrong about this one."

It took them almost a half hour to reach the house. It looked the same as Bobby remembered it from three years earlier. As he and Coffee approached the front door a chill ran down Bobby's spine. The house again was dark and silent. Coffee reached out to knock on front door, but his fist stopped in mid-air. The door was already slightly ajar. They both looked at each other as they each drew their pistols. Coffee pushed the door completely open.

"Mrs. Pololski, this is Captain Anderson. Are you there, Mrs. Pololski?"

When there was no answer, they cautiously made their way through the down stairs portion of the house to the kitchen located in the rear. There was still no sign of life.

"See, I told you, Bobby. You're paranoid."

Then they heard it. A crash came from one the rooms on the second floor.

"Pololski, if you're up there give yourself up. This isn't going to get you anywhere." Coffee yelled. He was standing beside the downstairs' banister. The house remained silent. Together, Bobby and Coffee ascended the stairs in crouched positions. Coffee lead. Bobby covered the rear. All but the door at the end of the upstairs landing were open. "Police!" Coffee yelled as he kicked the door open.

Mary Pololski's body was slumped over the writing desk in the far right corner of the bedroom. Her hand was only inches away from the phone. The front of her calico cotton dress was covered in blood. Her throat had been cut and her blood had begun to coagulate. It clung to the chair beneath her and continued to fall, drop by drop, into the pool that surrounded her feet.

"Christ!" Coffee exclaimed. "I really never thought . . ." He didn't get a chance to finish his sentence. A noise from the adjoining bathroom interrupted him.

Guns ready Bobby and Coffee gingerly pushed back the partially opened door. Sitting on the floor, next to the bath tub, was Samuel Pololski. He had slit both of his wrists. A broken bottle of Jack Daniels lay at his side.

Later after Walt had examined the bodies, he estimated that both had died between 4 and 5, almost the exact time Bobby had placed the call to Mary Pololski. They had been too late to save her. Coffee would always remember that day.

Walt was just finishing up his explanation of the five women's deaths. The blood had drained from Coffee's face.

"Holy Christ!" Coffee said as he walked over to where Bobby was standing. "We've got to get this guy and get him fast. If the papers get wind of this city's going to be in a panic. The information they already have is bad enough."

Bobby noticed the little beads of perspiration that were clinging to Coffee's forehead. "Let me put it to you this way Coffee. There are only eight people in this room that know exactly how these women died and five of them aren't talking." Bobby turned to leave. "I'm going downtown." he said. He stopped and turned back to face Coffee. "By the way, where's Kodak?"

"Oh you know how Kodak loves the morgue. I dropped him off at headquarters. He said the only kind of ribs he wanted to see were the kind covered in BBQ sauce." Coffee smiled.

Bobby hit the double doors with a little more force than necessary as he headed back in to the world of the living.

CHAPTER 7

Reporters circled Bobby, like Indians around a wagon train. Microphones and mini-cameras were shoved in his face as he fought his way up the front steps of headquarters.

"Is it true, Inspector Cash, that you have no significant leads in The Butcher Murders'?"

"No, it isn't true." The 'Butcher Murders, he thought. The press sure isn't at a loss for words when it comes to sensationalism. They're always looking for new angles to help sell papers. Well, the women of Chicago will sleep with one eye open tonight.

"Isn't true Inspector, that these women were not only horribly mutilated, but raped as well?"

"We have not received the final autopsy results yet."

"Inspector, we understand that these women have been dead for months and that if the electricity in the Argos Meat Packing House had not been shut off, the Chicago P.D. would still not even aware of the murders."

"As I said previously, the final results from the autopsies will give us an approximated time of death. We have not received those results yet. A formal statement will be made by the Coroner's Office when Dr. Barber's staff has concluded the examination of the victims."

"Have you identified any of the victims yet Inspector?"

"Identities of the women will be released to the press as soon as the next of kin have been notified."

"Then you do know who the dead women are?"

Before Bobby could answer, he heard a voice in the crowd ask, "How is it possible, Inspector, that with five brutal, unsolved murders on your hands, you can still find time for a two hour romantic lunch at the city's expense while this dement killer still stalks the streets?"

Even though the question had come from behind him, he didn't have to turn around to know who had asked it. He knew most of the reporters on the City staff. Most of them he liked. A few he didn't. Jane Dwyer, better known as eagle, was one of the reporters he didn't like.

Years ago they had been good friends. Her fiancé, Michael Mason, had been an anchor man at WGN-TV. He was Bobby's best, if not only friend. Jane had been the 'Eye in the Sky' traffic reporter. Michael and Bobby spent many nights drinking together into the wee hours of the morning, a habit Jane thoroughly disapproved of. One of their favorite haunts at the time was an old English Pub, the Town Crier. One night, at the Town Crier, when they were both well into their cups, Jane had came in looking for Michael. When she sat down to join them, Michael drunkenly slurred, "Well if my little Eagle hasn't landed." Disgusted with both of them and their behavior she left in a huff. Michael leaned over and clumsily whispered in Bobby's ear, "Everyone thinks I call her Eagle because she's a helicopter pilot and she has a reputation for being damn good at her job." He chuckled slightly. "But that's not the reason. I call her Eagle because of the way she can spread her legs!" They both doubled over with laughter and continued to laugh until the tears rolled down their faces. From that time on whenever anyone called her Eagle, Bobby had to hold back the temptation to snicker out loud. When she and Michael finally broke up Michael let her have it in the heated argument that pursued. He not only told her why he called her Eagle but he also told her that her that Bobby knew as well. From that day on she had hated Bobby's guts and she did everything she could to discredit him in the eyes of the public, as well as he superiors.

He turned to greet her with the biggest smile he could muster. The other reporters were aware that there was some sort of personal conflict between them, but not knowing the details, remained silent.

"Eagle, your information is as inaccurate as your nickname is accurate." He watched her face turn a bright crimson color. "I had a meeting with Patti Jacobs, who you well know, is a criminal physiologist and who's insight has been invaluable in a great many of our investigations. I suggest that if you have any misgivings about my abilities to head this investigation you take it up with the commissioner."

"I hope," she said, regaining some of her composure, "that you have more success in this homicide investigation than you did in the Davis case."

With that comment she succeeded in getting the rise out of Bobby she'd hoped for. Although his face remained completely composed, she could see the jugular vein on the side of his neck swell and redden.

"I have no further comments to make at this time!" he said as he glared at her. With that he wheeled around and continued up the remaining stairs into Headquarters.

"Bitch!" he muttered to himself as he stomped past the desk sergeant escaping into the sanctuary of the Homicide Department. The press was not allowed to follow him there.

The few detectives who remained on the floor sensed his mood as soon as he entered the squad room. They immersed themselves in their work in order to avoid the seething rage they sensed lay just beneath the calm exterior of their Chief Inspector.

Bobby could see Kodak, Dave Johnson and Detective Mike Hardy in his office. All three seemed to be engrossed in deep conversation. When Bobby entered his office he slammed the door so hard the glass shook. The smiles on their faces quickly disappeared as Bobby made his opening remark.

"What the fuck have you got and it better be good!" Kodak and Mike both looked at Dave to indicating to him he was the lucky one elected to disclose their findings.

"We've got identification on three of the women. One was Sharon Miles. She was a twenty-three year old who lived in the old town section with her boyfriend Allen Reese. Allen was the one who reported her missing. He said she had gone to an arts and crafts show. He didn't know where, since she was in the habit of going to a lot of them. She made pottery. She didn't come home. That was over two months ago. The second woman is Rose Peterson, age thirty-one. She lived with two roommates in the Lincoln Park area. The girls didn't talk to her the day she disappeared since they both went to work before Rose got up that morning. Rose had a night job and was still asleep when they left. They reported her missing the next day when the place she worked called to find out why she was not at work the night before. That was almost three months ago. The third woman was Jessica Ellis. She lived with her husband on the north side, off Lawrence Avenue. Her husband reported her missing when she didn't return from grocery shopping. He said he was sure that something had happened to her since she had never done anything like this before. He said their marriage was fine. She disappeared over a month ago. We don't know anything about the other two victims yet. Their fingerprints came up empty. We're still running a cross check on missing persons."

Dave handed Bobby the Missing Person files he had compiled on the three women. "The blood on the weapons in the cooler matches the blood types of all the victims. It's obvious they were the weapons used to take them apart, not that we doubted it." He reached down and brought up three plastic bags that had been laying on the floor. Each contained one of the weapons. He laid them all on Bobby's desk. "They were clean. He probably had gloves on because of the temperature in the cooler."

Bobby looked over at the weapons. "You might as well know that Walt thinks the women were alive when the guy cut them up. He said it was probably intentional."

Kodak, Dave and Mike each emitted different sounds of disgust and amazement as their eyes widened in horror.

"That information goes no further than this office. Got me?"

They nodded in agreement.

"Mike, run these pictures along with the names over to Walt and find out when he'll be ready for identification from the next of kin on these three. We can't have friends and relatives identifying body parts." He handed Mike the files. "Kodak and I will go over and talk to the Ellis husband. You and Townsend take the other two. Go over their places with a fine tooth comb. Let's see if we can find anything these three women might have had in common."

"I'm on my way! Oh, by the way Bobby, I got this from the old owners of the Argos Meat Packing Plant," He handed Bobby a sheet of paper. "It's a list of bidders they had on file from the liquidation sale. Anyone who bid was assigned a number. Maybe our killer was one of the bidders."

Bobby looked at the list. It amounted to fifteen or so names.

"Break it down between four or five men who aren't already tied up."

As soon as Dave and Mike left, Kodak spoke up for the first time. "How long it's been since you've been laid my man? You're so tense you couldn't get lucky with a fistful of fifties in a women's prison." He broke into a wide grin.

Bobby couldn't help but return the smile knowing it was Kodak's way of telling him to ease off.

"That's why you white boys die so young. You do too much fretting and not enough fucking."

A knock at the door kept Bobby from telling Kodak he'd been watching too many Oprah Winfrey shows. A very distinguished looking gray haired man cracked open the door and peered in. He was wearing gold rimmed glasses and a suit that probably cost at least five hundred dollars Bobby guessed.

"Inspector Cash?"

"Shit!" Bobby thought. "Who's suing me now?"

"That's me." Bobby responded. "What can I do for you?"

"My name is Howard Bissell." He held his hand out for Bobby to shake. "I have some business to discuss with you."

He looked over at Kodak. "Privately, if you don't mind."

Kodak, knowing how to take a hint quickly picked up the three plastic bags containing the weapons and said, "I'll take these back to the evidence room."

After Kodak left Bissell put the briefcase he was carrying on his lap and opened it.

"Now, what's this all about?" Bobby questioned as Bissell shuffled through the papers in his case.

"Before I tell you, I have to ask you some questions. Is your full name Robert Allen Cash, son of Harold and Lucille Cash?"

"Yes, but what . . ."

"Please, Inspector Cash be patient and I'll explain fully. Was your mother's maiden name McElinney, daughter of Stanley and Kathleen McElinney?"

"Yes."

"And were you born January first, 1938? Is that correct?"

"Yes!" Bobby was getting slightly irritated by all the mystery.

"Well, Inspector Cash, I have some good news for you. Mrs. McElinney past away about a month ago and you are now the sole benefactor of her estate."

"My grandmother? I haven't seen her since I was probably seven years old. Why would she leave me her estate?"

"I don't know the reasons Inspector Cash. All I can tell you is that as of this moment you're a very wealthy man."

"You mean their farm was valuable?"

"Farm, Inspector Cash? I know nothing about a farm."

"But when I was a child they lived on a farm somewhere close to the Illinois-Wisconsin Border."

"That might have been true when you were a child but her current address is in Lake Forest on Sheridan Road. The house alone is worth in the neighborhood of six hundred thousand dollars."

"Some neighborhood!" Bobby exclaimed with a low whistle. He couldn't quite believe what he was hearing.

"The total net worth of the estate is approximately three million dollars."

"Three million dollars!" Where would my grandmother get that kind of money?" He knew there had to be some sort of mistake. There must be another Bobby Cash out there for whom all this was really intended.

"Your grandfather was a long-time friend of Ray Krock," Bissell said interrupting Bobby's thoughts.

"McDonald's Ray Krock?" Bobby asked.

"One and the same. At one time they were both salesmen for the sterling Multi-Products Company. Even though Mr. Krock left the company he and your grand father kept in close contact. When Mr. Krock came up with the idea for McDonalds your grandfather invested heavily in the company. As McDonalds grew, so did your grandfather's fortune. When he died eight years ago he left everything to his wife, your grandmother. She in turn left everything to you."

Bobby was speechless.

"I understand from Ms. Nicole Jadot, who by the way, is your partner in the French restaurant, Le Fleur, in Lincolnshire . . ."

"What restaurant?"

"I'll get to that in a second. Anyway Ms. Jadot was a long time friend and companion of your grandmother, as well as her business associate. She told me that your parents had a falling out with your grandparent years ago when you where still very young. According to her, in all these years, no effort was ever made to reconcile their differences.

"That, I know is true." Bobby said. "When my parents were alive they never even mentioned my grandparents. I remember the couple of times my grandmother did call the house, my father slammed the phone down refusing to talk to her."

"About the restaurant. Ms. Jadot and your grandmother were partners, so now you are Ms. Jadot's partner. Ms. Jadot by the way lives in the coach house on your grandmother's estate. I guess now I should say, your estate. It's up to you to decide whether or not you want her to vacate premises. You'll need to discuss that issue with her. Since it's getting late," he glanced at his watch, "I suggest you to meet me at the estate tomorrow if possible. At that time we can go over all of the assets."

Bobby, whose head was swimming with the news of his unexpected fortune, could only mutter. "Where? When?"

"How about 10:00 A.M.? Is that time convenient for you?"

"Yes, fine. Just fine." He was having a hard time putting sentences together.

"The address is 2222 Sheridan Road. I'll see you there at 10:00 A.M." He put the papers back in his briefcase, shook Bobby's hand and was gone before Bobby had a chance to return to earth.

Kodak must have said, "Bobby" three times before he got any response. "For a second there I though you'd gone comatose on me. What did that guy want with you anyway, if you don't mind my asking?"

Bobby looked up form his desk. he was wearing the best 'cat eating the canary' grin Kodak had ever seen.

"Kodak, before we go over to the Ellis place, I'm going to buy you the biggest and best steak dinner in the city of Chicago."

"Am I hearing you right? You're going to buy me a steak dinner? You, the king of the Big Mac and a large order of fries?"

Bobby laughed. "Yup, me, the Big Mac and large order of fries king." There was no way for Kodak to mow the truth that lay beneath that statement.

"What do you say? How about Geonetti's?"

Kodak's eyes opened wide in disbelief. Geonetti's was the best steak house in town. "Let's get out of here before you change your mind.

CHAPTER 8

The jovial mood that prevailed through dinner vanished as soon Bobby and Kodak reached the front steps of the Ellis home. They waited patiently as Peter Ellis opened the front door. The look in his eyes told them he already knew why they were here. His voice even cracked when he asked them to come in.

"Mr. Ellis," Bobby began. "we've come to inform you . . ."

"You don't' have to tell me." he said as he picked up the evening paper. "She's one of them!" He pointed to the headlines: FIVE WOMEN FOUND BUTCHERED. "Isn't she?"

"I'm afraid she is Mr. Ellis."

"Oh my God!" He covered his face with his hands and began to cry, softly at first and then harder and harder until his entire body was racked by deep, uncontrollable sobs.

Kodak and Bobby waited until he had regained his composure before they asked him any further questions. "Mr. Ellis I know this is very difficult for you, but we'd like you, if you're able, to answer some questions about the day your wife disappeared."

Peter Ellis wiped his tear stained face with the back of his hand. "I understand." he said, nodding his head. "I want you to get the bastard! Whoever he is!" Anger and hatred filled his voice. He sat down heavily on the couch and motioned for Kodak and Bobby to sit in the matching barrel chairs.

"Saturdays were always Jessie's day to shop. During the week she worked full-time as a legal secretary for Cohen and Cohen, a law firm on Lasalle Street. The Saturday she disappeared we had both slept later than usual. The previous night we went to a dinner party that didn't break up until well after midnight. Both of us had more to drink than we should have. Saturday morning Jessie got up first. I stayed in bed while she showered and dressed. When she finished she knelt on the bed beside me, kissed me on the forehead and told me that she was going shopping and would probably stop by and see her mother while she was out. That was the last that I saw her." Tears were streaming down his face.

"I loved her so much! We've only been married two years." Unable to hold back his grief any longer, he dropped his head and sobbed like a frightened, small child. Bobby and Kodak sat helplessly, as they had so many times before, as they watched the loved ones of the victim become yet another type of victim of the killer.

Kodak pointed to the wedding picture that sat on top of the television set. They both looked so happy and full of promise in the photograph. Her eyes were so alive. Her face beamed with joy and love as she looked into the face of her new husband. It was not at all the face Bobby had seen the morning they found the victims. That face had been blank and unfeeling as it lay on the cold concrete floor of the meat locker.

"I'm sorry," Peter Ellis said. "I just can't believe it . . ."

Bobby interrupted. "It's all right Mr. Ellis. We understand, we just had a few more questions."

Kodak stood up.

"Mr. Ellis, is it all right if Detective Webster looks around?" Bobby continued.

Peter Ellis looked puzzled by the request but shrugged his shoulders in consent. Bobby continued his questioning as Kodak wandered from room to room.

"What grocery store did your wife shop at?"

"Her favorites were either Dominic's on Lawrence, which is about six blocks from here, or Treasure Island on Milwaukee Avenue in Hamlet Square."

"Did you know which store she was going to on the day she disappeared?"

"No." his mouth quivered. "It didn't seem important enough at the time to ask."

"What about her mother. Where does she live?"

"Last year we put her in the Pleasant Arms Rest Home over on Halstead Street. She has Alzheimer's disease and can't take care of herself. Jess would try to visit her at least twice a month."

"Where on Halstead Street is the home located?"

"I don't know the exact address. I can look it up for you if you want though."

"No that's all right Mr. Ellis. We'll get it. What is the name of your wife's mother?"

"Blanch Less."

Bobby noticed that Kodak had finished his inspection of the house. "If you can think of anything else that might help us, call me at this number." He handed Peter Ellis his card. "And one more thing. I'm sorry but you'll have to go down to the morgue tomorrow to officially identify your wife's body."

Horror filled Peter Ellis eyes. He thought of having to see his wife's dead body hadn't occurred to him. He stood speechless as Bobby and Kodak let themselves out.

Kodak was the first to break the silence as they sat in the darkness of the squad car. Both of them could still feel the depth of despair that lay behind the walls of the house they had just left.

"I found no sign of violence. No dented walls or doors. No busted doors jams or windows. I'd say the guy is on the level."

"What did you find out about her?" Bobby asked as he started the car.

"There were two racquet ball trophies in the den and a plaque for 'employee of the month' from the law firm where she worked. A lighted cabinet contained a display of paper weights. Some of them had cards next to them with the names of David Lotton and William Manson the designers. She had quite a nice collection. Her closet was as neat as a pin. It was even coordinated by the color of her garments. It looked as if she had every intention of coming back."

"Ellis said she was going to stop in and visit her mother at the Pleasant Arms Rest Home on Halstead Street. I want you to go over in the morning and check it out. I've got some private business to attend to in the morning. I'll meet you back at headquarters as soon as I can. Tell Coffee to set up a meeting for around 3:00 P.M. I want all of the detectives to attend."

For the remainder of the ride Bobby and Kodak talked very little and even though they didn't know it they were both sharing the same thoughts. They both desperately wanted the killer caught. They both wanted to spare anyone else the pain that Peter Ellis was feeling. They were both thinking of the stiff drink they would pour for themselves when they got home, hoping that it would help numb the pain they were feeling and allow them to get, at least, some sleep.

Instead of taking the Morgue direct route on his grandmother's estate in Lake Forest the next morning Bobby decided to take the outer drive that wound alone the shore of Lake Michigan. The waves lapped against the battered seawall had a calming effect on him. He drove slower than the 45 M.P.H. posted speed signs that lined the picturesque skyline. Boats of every size, shapes and colors filled the various harbors along the way and dotted the horizon for as far as he could see.

Bobby's father had been the captain of an iron ore freighter on the Great Lakes. He assumed he must have inherited his love of the sea from him. Every summer the company would allow his mother and him to accompany his father on the ship for a month as his father went from port to port loading and unloading iron ore. In his youth he had never appreciated those months. At the time it had meant leaving his friends for most of the summer. But now, as a man, he would give his ride arm to be going out on one of those ships again. He was only fifteen years old when his father was lost at sea in a violent storm on Lake Superior. Bobby never really forgave his father for leaving him with the burden and the responsibility of taking care of his mother who required constant supervision.

He used to escape to Belmont Harbor when problems weighed too heavily on his young mind. The sea had always been able to offer him the solace and the comfort he needed, even if his escape was only for the day and although he didn't realize it he was looking for the same type of therapy today.

Bobby accelerated and left the lake behind to make his way through the congested suburbs of the city. He finally reached the sprawling and affluent suburb of Lake Forest and found Sheridan Road which twisted through old fashioned Gatsby like estates and free flowing glass and stone, contemporary ones.

As he approached 2222 Sheridan he noticed the estate fell somewhere in between the old fashioned 1920's and the more contemporary 1980 style estates. The long graceful driveway was marked simply by two white stucco columns located on either side of the driveway. Both columns were about five feet high and each was adorned with a statue shaped like a pineapple. The large oak trees that lined either side of the driveway formed an archway that lead to the house. The branches of the trees were intertwined so densely the sun's rays almost completely blocked from view. At the end of the line of trees the driveway circled in front of the large, white, two story English Tudor Style house. The house was surrounded with shrubs and flower gardens that were already bursting with spring blooms. Bobby pulled up behind the white, late model Mercedes parked at the front entrance and stared at the stately home that now belonged to him.

Howard Bissell opened the front door to greet Bobby even before he was half way up the front steps. "Inspector Cash, please do come in." He held the door wide open to admit Bobby into a large foyer. The center of the foyer contained an old ornate oak table on which sat an expensive looking crystal vase. The vase had been artistically filled with freshly cut flowers.

"Because I have previous appointments today and my time, I'm sorry to say, is limited, I suggest we get right to the business at hand. Afterwards you can take your time to familiarize yourself with the house and grounds. I have all the necessary papers in the library, if you'll please follow me."

They walked through the large double doors of the foyer and into the type of room Bobby imagined was built for men to have brandy and cigars after dinner. The walls were lined with leather bound books. The sofa and chairs were covered in a worn, but rich brown leather. A brick fireplace separated the couch and chairs from the mahogany, leather-embossed desk and chair that was located on the other side of the room.

Howard Bissell's opened briefcase sat on the coffee table that at one time had been a hatch door on a ship. Bobby and Howard sat,almost simultaneously on the couch in front of it. Howard Bissell handed Bobby a piece of paper and said, "This is a list of the assets your grandmother left you. The list includes this house, which is completely paid for, a bank account with $348,653.83 on deposit, 30,000 shares of McDonald's stock and half ownership of the restaurant 'Le Fleur'. The bank account and the stock have already been transferred into your name. According to yesterday's price on the stock market your stock is worth a little over 2 million dollars. The restaurant has a fifteen year mortgage. It grossed almost 1 million dollars last year and is doing quite nicely thanks to Ms. Jadot, who by the way is the partner in the business and in my opinion it would be a mistake to sell your fifty percent share of the restaurant."

"I just can't believe it!" Bobby said shaking his head. "I had no idea my grandparents were this wealthy. Now that it's mine . . ." His voice trailed off as he continued to stare at the list he held on his hands.

"I have some papers here for you to sign." Bissell said as he pushed the documents in front of Bobby and handed him his gold Cross pen.

"What exactly am I signing?" He hadn't been a cop all these years for nothing.

"Simply, that I, our firm as the executor of your grandmother's estate have fulfilled our obligations in locating you and informing you of her estate and that we have signed over the ownership, less a deduction for our fee, to you."

Bobby smiled at Howard Bissell before he finally picked up the pen and signed the documents. He didn't think Bissell was going to all this trouble out of the goodness of his heart.

He signed the document in three places and initialized in two others.

Bissell put the papers back in his briefcase and stood up. He glanced at his watch as he said, "I think we should walk over to the coach house to see Ms. Jadot now. Then, I'm afraid I must leave you, by the way, before you can use any of the funds, you must go to the Lake Forest First National Bank and register your signature. A Mr. Bill Edwards is expecting you."

Bobby, who has still in a daze, followed Bissell out the front door past the garages and over to the separate driveway leading to the coach home at the back of the estate.

Nicole Jadot did not come to the door to let Bissell and Bobby in. Instead she yelled, "Come in. Come in. The door's open."

They entered the large one room coach house that she had converted into a unique home for herself. Bobby thought the room could have easily been photographed for the cover of House Beautiful. Since the Japanese screen she used as a wall partition at the front entrance blocked their view of the kitchen where her voice was coming from, they could only walk in the direction of it. When they reached the kitchen they understood why she had not greeted them at the door. Her back was facing them and she was bent over the natural colored Mexican tile counter, busily engaged in something they could not see.

"I'll be with you in a minute. Sit down. There's coffee and cups on the counter. Help yourself." Her long brown hair swayed back and forth as she continued whatever it was she was doing, not breaking her concentration.

Bobby and Bissell sat at the tiled breakfast counter. The blue, plaid cushions, made the brown wicker bar stools very comfortable. Bissell poured both himself and Bobby a cup of coffee as Nicole had suggested. From where the two of them sat they could see that Nicole was making chocolate pie shells. The hot melted chocolate dried quickly as she skillfully swirled it across the bottom and up the sides of the wax paper lined molds. She carried the finished product over to the refrigerator. When she opened the door they could see that it contained at least another dozen chocolate shells.

"Well," she said washing her hands and turning around, "this must be my new partner." She held out her hand.

Bobby stared at her as if he were in a trance. She was perhaps, the most beautiful woman he had ever seen. Her huge, dark brown eyes smiled kindly at him. Her soft rose-colored lips accentuated her high cheekbones and light olive complexion.

Aware of his reaction to her, she laughed and said, "Don't worry Mr. Cash, I won't put you to work in the kitchen."

Bobby immediately relaxed and said, "If you want to keep your customers, you won't. And please call me Bobby." He smiled.

Bissell's voice made Bobby release her hand. "Ms. Jadot, I would like to leave Mr. Cash in your capable hands." Bobby smiled at the pleasant prospect. "I'm afraid I'm in a hurry and haven't really got the time to show him the house and the grounds and of course the restaurant."

"If Mr. Cash, I mean Bobby has the time, I'd be happy to." She looked at him for his response.

"I can't think of anyone's hands I'd rather be put into. Thank you."

With that, Bissell stood, made his apologies and left. Bobby and Nicole sat awkwardly for a few moments after he had left. Neither knew quite what to say to the other. Nicole was the first to break the silence. She looked down at herself and then murmured, "Well, if you'll give me a few moments to change, I'll take you on the grand tour."

"Sounds good to me." Bobby replied.

"Good, I'll be just a minute." Nicole walked behind him and disappeared up the open stairway that led to the loft and to her bedroom. She talked to him as she changed her clothes. "I understand you're a cop. Oh, I'm sorry. I meant a policeman."

"That's OK. I've been called worse than that. Yea, I'm Inspector of Homicide for the Chicago P.D."

"Sounds very impressive. How long have you been doing that?"

About twenty-three years".

"You're in charge of that investigation on those five murdered women they found, aren't you?"

The phone interrupted and kept Bobby from answering her. "Excuse me". She said.

Bobby surveyed the room while she talked on the upstairs phone. At the far end of the coach house a massive stone fireplace covered the wall from floor to ceiling. A white overstuffed traditional sectional sat in front of the fireplace. Plants and an antique wooden cigar Indian decorated one of the plank walls. A table, large enough for twelve people, sat in the center of the room. The buffet was decorated with gargoyles and stained glass which reflected the light from the skylights above and cast a prism of color across the table. The walls were covered with old signs and prints. Baskets of various sizes filled with straw flowers sat on the floor. The room was warm and inviting like, he assumed, the woman who designed and occupied it was.

"I'm ready". She said as she came back down the stairs. She wore an ankle length tan skirt with a matching blouse. Her outfit was accented with a turquoise and silver belt and brown leather boots. She had piled her hair loosely on top of her head. Little curly wisps of hair framed her face and neck. She was even lovelier now than when he had first seen her. He felt himself staring again.

"What would you like to see first?" she said, stepping close to him. He could smell the soft delicate scent of her perfume.

"You're the tour guide. Just lead the way."

CHAPTER 9

C offee rolled out the huge map of Chicago while Bobby set up the chalk board. As Coffee stuck colored pins in the locations of the meat locker and the homes of the murdered victims Bobby divided the chalk board into five sections. Each section represented a victim and listed their name and the names of those they lived with. A question mark was placed in the sections for the two unidentified victims. When Bobby finished he turned to address the detectives who gathered in a semicircle around him.

"As you are aware, we only know the identity of three of the victims. Today pictures of the other two women have been released to the press in the hope that someone will come forward and identify them. Of the three victims we have identified, we still know very little. As you can see from the map none of the women lived close to the meat locker." He picked up a pointer. "Victim number one, Sharon Miles, lived all the way over in Old Town. Rose Peterson, victim number two, lived in Lincoln Park and victim number three lived on the far north side. Assuming that they all, for some reason, strayed into the assailant's territory and not the other way around, we are going to concentrate our investigation within a two mile radius of the meat locker."

One of the detectives interjected. "But what if you're wrong and he grabbed his victims close to their homes them we'd just be wasting our time and giving the killer more time."

"We have one good piece of evidence that leads us to believe he killed his victims close to the Meat Locker. Kodak, tell them what you've got." All eyes turned towards the back of the room where Kodak stood.

"Inspector Cash and I interrogated Mr. Ellis at his home last night. His wife, Jessica, victim number three, disappeared about a month ago on a Saturday. She never returned form her grocery shopping trip. The original missing persons report didn't mention the fact that she had planned to visit her mother that same day. This morning, I checked out the rest home where her mother is confined. The rest home is located on Halstead Street. Jessica Ellis' mother has Alzheimer's disease and could not verify her daughter's visit but a day nurse, Sue Carter, did remember the visit. Ms. Carter told me that Jessica arrived around noon that day. She stayed and had lunch with her mother in the main dining room. Her mother threw a tantrum in the dining room and had to be restrained by two orderlies. Ms. Carter gave her an injection to sedate her and then returned with the orderlies and Jessica Ellis. When they took her mother back to her room, Ms. Carter said that Jessica broke down and cried that she comforted her for a good half hour. Then Jessica left. She also claimed that Jessica said she was going to browse around some of the shops in area for about an hour before stopping back to check on her mother before going home. But according to Ms. Carter, Jessica never returned for that second visit."

Bobby picked up where Kodak had left off. "We are assuming the killer nabbed her somewhere in this vicinity." He pointed at the map once more. "As you can see it's only a few miles from the meat locker where she was found." His pointer circled the two locations. "That's why I want to concentrate our investigation in the area around Halstead Street. I think that Sharon Miles and Rose Peterson, for one reason or another, were also in that area and I want to find out why they were there and exactly where they were. That tells us something about Jessica Ellis. Mike, what did you find out about Sharon Miles?"

"She was born and raised a Chicago girl. She came from a low income family who lived on the south side. She moved out on her own at the age of fifteen. She has a record of juvenile arrest for disorderly conduct. She met her boyfriend at a peace rally three years ago. They've been living together ever since. To support themselves, he waits on tables at the Lion's Den, a burger place in Old Town, and she makes and sells pottery. The day she disappeared she was going to an art and crafts show to sell her wares. He doesn't know where. According to him she went to a lot of them. She was driving an old V.W. van that's never been found. That's about it." Mike sat back down.

"There may have been an arts and craft show in the area that we're concentrating our search in." Bobby turned toward Townsend. "What did you find out about the Peterson woman?"

Art Townsend shook his head as he stood up. "You guys found out a hell of a lot more than I did. Rose Peterson kept to herself. Her roommates knew very little about her personal habits. She been married once, she was very young, for about five years. She was the night manager at the downtown Hilton. Her boss says she was personable and very competent at her job. Most of the times she worked six days a week. When I checked her room I found nothing out of the ordinary. She has a hobby of collecting figurines that were made in occupied Japan. She had a cabinet full of that stuff. Her roommates said she wasn't dating anyone at the time, that they were aware of. We're trying to locate her old boyfriend. He moved to California about a year ago. So far, we can't find anyone who saw or talked to her on the day she disappeared. As far as we know, she has no living relatives." Art sat back down.

Coffee spoke up for the first time. "The detectives who have been assigned to work the meat locker neighborhood have had very little luck. They haven't been able to find anything. Most of the people who live there, both husbands and wives, work so the homes are mostly empty during the day. No one remembers anything unusual going on over there at night." Coffee walked over to a desk and picked up a manila envelope. "There is one woman, a Jan Arneson, who said her car wouldn't start a few weeks ago. Her battery seemed to be dead so she called the local gas station for a tow truck to come out and give her a jump since her husband had already left for the office. She was waiting in the driveway for the tow truck when she noticed a blue pick-up truck pull around the back of the Argos Meat Packing Plant. She said that she really didn't pay much attention to it since she was thinking about being late for work."

Kodak broke in. "A blue pick-up was in the line of traffic yesterday. Maybe it's the same one."

Coffee continued. "Could be Kodak, but there's hundreds of blue pickups running around this town. That isn't much to go on."

"As you said," Bobby interjected, looking at Coffee, "it may just be coincidence, but I think Kodak and I will go back and talk to the Arneson woman one more time. Maybe she can remember something else. And what about the gas station guy? He might have seen something."

Coffee started to stutter. "Um, huh . . . . I don't think so." His face began to flush. "Bobby you're just blowing smoke up your ass."

Bobby hated that term. He turned to Coffee and through clenched teeth growled, "that may be, but unless you've got any better leads to follow, I'm willing to blow a little smoke and follow these leads." He then turned his attention back to the detectives in front of him. "Anyone got any questions or comments?"

Mike Hardy stood back up. "That list we got at the auction. Well, so far nothing. We'll keep at it though."

Bobby asked for further comments, but none were presented. "OK, if that's it, you all know where you're headed. Get on it."

They talked among themselves as Coffee issued new assignments to some of them. The detectives who were already assigned, paired up with their partners and left to pick up the investigation where they had left off. Bobby and Kodak walked into Bobby's office. The phone was ringing. Bobby grabbed it.

"Cash," he said as he sat down. "Hi Walt. What can I do for you?"

"Just about everything," Walt laughed. "Besides getting less than three hours of sleep in the last twenty four hours and going without breakfast or dinner last night, Peter Ellis just collapsed in the viewing room. When I tried to help him to his feet, he upchucked all over me. Let me tell you, I've had better days!"

"We saw the Ellis kid last night. He wasn't in the greatest shape then. He was taking it real hard. Can't say I blame him."

"Why does it always happen to the good ones."

Bobby sighed. "It's a bitch, Walt. A real bitch!"

"The reason I called, Bobby, is that we came up with some more information on you killer."

"That's great!" Bobby said excitedly. "What did you get?"

"We got lucky on the sperm left in the vaginal canal and on hair we picked up from all the victims. We know he's a Caucasian male between the age of thirty-five and forty-five. He has black hair and his blood type is O negative. How's that?"

"Walt, if I were gay, I'd probably ask you out." They both laughed.

"Don't let that stop you. I'm up for almost anything, except maybe Kodak. He reminds me of the kind who kisses and tells."

Bobby looked over at Kodak. "I've got all the preliminary results. Enough information to sooth the savage beasts."

"I'll set it up for 11:00 A.M. How's that."

"That's just fine. I'll see you then."

"Uh, Walt, before you hang up. Don't forget, no reference to the fact that the victims were probably alive during part of the mutilation."

"Gotcha!" Walt hung up.

Jan Arneson was a plain looking woman and not at all thrilled with the prospect of being questioned again by the police.

"As I told the other detective who already questioned me, I was really in a hurry that morning and all I remember is a blue pick-up truck. That's all." She started to close the front door.

Bobby pushed it back open. "Mrs. Arneson, we can do this the easy way or the hard way. You can talk to us now. Here. Or we can go (down town). Now which is it going to be?"

She sighed. "O.K. But really, that's all I know."

"What about the pick-up? Was there any writing or dents on it? Anything unusual?"

She stood quietly for a moment trying to recall that morning. She began to shake her head and started to say "no." Then she stopped and said, "Wait a minute. There was something. The back of the truck was made of wood."

"Wood, Mrs. Arneson?"

"Yes. You know. Wooden sides."

Kodak and Bobby looked at each other. "Thank you Mrs. Arneson. You've been a big help." They walked down the sidewalk and got back into the squad car.

"That's the same truck. I'd lay money on it." Kodak said.

"Before we get too excited here, let's go over to the Texaco station that sent the tow truck and check with the driver to see if he saw anything."

"But Bobby," Kodak said. "it all fits. Walt said the guy had black hair and was around thirty-five years old. The guy I saw driving that truck matches the description."

"Could be Kodak. Could be."

It took about twenty minutes for Harold, of Harold's Texaco station, to search through his last month's receipts to locate the charge for the Arneson woman's jump and to identify the driver who had responded to the call.

"Here it is," Harold said. "Eddie Mitchell was the driver. He's out on a call right now but I expect him back any minute."

Bobby and Kodak waited. When Harold arrived he remembered the call.

"Oh, you mean the dame that lived across the street from where all those women was found butchered. Yea, I remember giving her a jump, with the tow truck that is. The woman's no looker." Eddie smiled, but Bobby didn't smile back. "Yea, let me see. Yea, I remember a blue pick-up truck. Mrs. Arneson's car started right up once I connected the cables. I gave her the bill and waited while she wrote me a check. When I backed my rig out of her driveway, I waited for her to drive away. Guess I blocked the street a little. Anyway, I'm watching her go down the block when this maniac behind me starts blowing his horn and yelling obscenities at me like I've been sitting there for an hour or something. I look in my rear view mirror and it's this nut in a blue pick-up truck."

"Can you tell me what he looked like?" Bobby asked.

"Nah, I can't really remember. It was too long ago. Except, I do remember he had a beard. A black beard."

Kodak broke into a big smile. He could feel it in his bones. This was the guy.

Bobby issued an all points bulletin on the blue pick-up and a general description of their primary suspect. Things were looking up. So he thought.

"It's me. I've got some information for you."

"What is it?"

"It's worth a little more than usual. A hundred bucks more."

"Tell me what it is and well see."

Jane Dwyer smiled to herself. Tomorrow's headlines would read, 'WOMEN ALIVE WHEN BUTCHERED. SUSPECT SOUGHT!'

CHAPTER 10

L
e Fleur was located about fifteen minutes off of the Tri-State Expressway on the outskirts of Lincolnshire. Even though it was late, the parking lot was still full of cars, most of which belonged to the upper crust the Lincolnshire area was noted for.

The trees that surrounded the old, renovated farm house were strung with small, white Christmas tree lights. The lights could be seen long before you reached the restaurant. The grounds reminded Bobby of the old Villa Venice on Milwaukee Avenue in Wheeling, Illinois. As a student at Lane Tech High School in Chicago, he and his buddies had gone there for dinner and dancing after the junior senior prom. The gondolas there were great for romantic rides up and down the Des Plaines River which bordered one side of the property. For a price, the gondolier would look the other way as bras were unsnapped and zippers undone in a hurried scramble for a twenty minute, uninterrupted session of heavy petting, before they had to return to the ballroom and the watchful eyes of the school's chaperons.

Bobby pulled the unmarked police car under the green and white striped canopy. A wooden sign in the driveway read, 'Valet Parking.' A young man came out from behind the closed double French doors and said, "I'm sorry sir, but we're closed for the evening."

"I'm here to see Ms. Jadot," Bobby replied as he got out of the car.

"Yes sir," the young man said looking up at Bobby. "She's right inside."

Bobby smiled, pulled a five dollar bill from his pocket, handed it to the boy and said, "Take good care of my car. I wouldn't want anything to happen to it."

The young man rolled his eyes and lifted his eyebrows in a gesture to depict the complete absurdity of Bobby's statement. He couldn't imagine anyone wanting to steal that poor excuse of a car when the lot was full of expensive foreign imports to choose from.

When Bobby entered the restaurant, he stood at the hostess podium and looked around the dining room. He realized that if he had come with the intention of dining, he was improperly dressed. Everyone in the restaurant was all 'decked-up' as his father used to say. A couple of men even wore tuxedo style jackets and the women who accompanied them glittered from the diamonds and other precious stones that adorned their ears and throats. The room itself was a mass of color and warmth. The carpet and the walls were somewhere between mauve and a dusty rose color. The tables were covered with floral pattern tablecloths that presented a soft hue of pinks, blues and burgundies. The entire scene reminded him of a Renoir painting. The candles in the crystal candlestick holders flickered and sent a flattering light across each table.

Bobby looked around, but could not spot Nicole so he walked across the hall to one of the other dining rooms. This room contrasted starkly with the other room. Instead of a floral motif, this room was decorated with plaids of beiges, browns and baby blues. These colors dominated the room. Bobby thought he would be more comfortable dining here.

A waiter, who noticed Bobby in the doorway, walked over to him asked, "Yes sir. May I help you?"

"I'm looking for Ms.Jadot."

"I believe she is upstairs in the lounge," the waiter said motioning in the direction of the staircase at the end of the hall.

Bobby thanked him and walked up the stairs to enter the open room that occupied the entire second floor. A large wood and brass octagon bar sat in the center of the room. Cabinets with wire mesh doors hung from the ceiling and contained every imaginable liqueur and liquor made. Comfortable, overstuffed sofas and chairs were arranged in small, intimate groupings. Huge porthole—type windows offered and unobstructed view of the small lake and the surrounding woods that had been subtly lit with selectively placed spot lights. The dark paneled walls were covered with nautical memorabilia. Everything from the engine room lights and whaler's old time harpoons to bronze props and glass and hemp lobster pot floats adorned the walls. When Bobby sat down at the empty bar, he felt as if he were sitting in the main saloon of windjammer instead of the lounge of a restaurant.

The bartender was a large man, somewhere in his fifties. He had the pug nose of a prize fighter. The buttons on his black vest strained to conceal the prominent belly beneath. He shoved a cocktail napkin in front of Bobby as he said, "Hi. What can I get for you?"

"How about a Grant's on the rocks with a twist," Bobby replied. He smelled Nicole's fragrance even before he felt her hand on his shoulder.

"Make that two, Big John."

Bobby turned to face Nicole. She smiled at him and said to the bartender, "Big John, I'd like you to meet Bobby Cash.

He's my new partner and your new boss so you'd better be good to him."

Big john put the drinks down in front of Bobby and Nicole, extended his large hand, shook Bobby's hand and said, "It's a good to meet you sir."

"None of that 'sir' stuff Big John. Just Bobby will do and don't let Nicole scare you. I may be her new partner but the only orders I'll be giving, is to pour me a drink. And from looking at the size of you, I'm going to say please."

Big John smiled. "You're not exactly a dwarf yourself. Anything that I can do to help out, you just ask."

Big John has been with me and this establishment since day one. He's the cornerstone of this place. I don't know what I would have done without him."

The dim light in the room helped, but didn't quite conceal, the blush of pleasure that spread across Big John's face.

"It was nice meeting you Bobby. Now if you'll both excuse me, I've got a bar to restock. If I don't get it done the owners of this joint will probably have my hide." He winked at Nicole, turned and left through the opening at the back of the bar.

Nicole shook her head and smiled. "He's a treasure."

"This is a pretty impressive place you've got here." Bobby said. "Who decorated it anyway?"

"Thank—you. Your grandmother and I did most of it. Did you get a chance to look around?"

"When I came in, I looked into the dining rooms. It's definitely the kind of place you'd want to bring your best girl."

"And do you have a best girl, Bobby?"

"No, I'm sorry to say, I don't. Cops don't exactly have the kind of lifestyle that's conductive for long term relationships. What about you? Have you found that certain someone?"

"I did once. Or I thought I had. I was young and impulsive. I thought marriage was forever. My ex-husband thought it was for uncomplicated one night stands. 'C'est la vie' as they say. Now, let's get off his depressing subject." She raised her drink. "Here's to you, me, and Le Fleur." Their glasses clinked in a toast as they looked into each others eyes.

"Nickel?" a waiter at the top of the stairs broke the spell between them. "The Harrington's are leaving now and they wish to say good-bye."

"I'll be right down." Nicole rose from her seat and looked at Bobby. "I'll only be a moment."

"That's all right. I'd better be going myself anyway."

"Please don't go. That is, if you don't have to. We've got a lot to talk about. After all, it isn't every day a person gets a new partner and a new landlord all in one crack.

Bobby looked at her. He didn't think he could deny her anything.

Before he could answer, Nicole said, "Big John, would you please make Bobby and me another drink. Then you can close if you want."

"Sure thing Nickel." Big John stopped what he was doing and made two fresh drinks. Bobby watched Nicole as she descended the stairs. Her black, floor-length gown clung seductively to her tall, lean body.

"Did I hear you right?" Big John laughed. "When we first opened, our chef, Jean Paul, had an assistant, Joe, who could not pronounce Nicole. He would say Nickel instead. Somehow the name stuck. Now even our steady customers call her Nickel."

"I'm glad you cleared that up for me Big John. I thought I was losing my hearing."

Just then Nicole rejoined them at the bar.

"And speaking of hearing, "he said turning to face her, "want to hear how you got the idea for this room. Where in the world did you get all of this old, nautical stuff for the walls?"

"Before I bore you with all the details, let's get comfortable." Nicole led him to the set of sofas that stood in front of the porthole windows. She sat down, took her shoes off, pulled her legs up underneath her, and started to massage her toes with her fingers. "Oh, that's better," she said. The small ship's lantern on the table between them sent a soft glow across the room and cast shadows that enhanced her dark, exotic features. "My father was a carpenter. He could perform miracles with wood. When I was very small, we moved from Quebec to the town of Lake Geneva, in Wisconsin. My father's brother had lived there for years. He asked my father to go into business with him. They started the business of J&J Contractors which specialized in building custom homes. They were quite successful. Anyway, my father had one passion. Sailboats. Lake Geneva is one of the best lakes in the country for sailing. I understand some Olympic medallists even learned how to sail there. Anyway, in his spare time, what little he had, he built from scratch, a twenty-three foot sloop. He christened her 'Le Fleur', the flower. Whenever my father considered something or someone perfect, he would say they or it was the flower. The best. Perfect. Hence, that's were I got the name for the restaurant. Well, in the winter when there was little work and he couldn't sail, he would carve model ships. Only these ships weren't small models. They would sometimes be five or six feet long. They would open up, like the back of a doll house, to reveal every miniature detail of the luxury yacht they were modeled after. He made everything from engines to wood furniture for the saloons. This room came from his imagination. It is decorated like one of the saloons from his favorite ship. He called her, "Multum In Parvo". It means 'Much in little'. She was his favorite. And mine."

"Did your father build this room?" Bobby asked.

"No. He died years ago. This room reminds me of him though. I know he would have loved it. As for the nautical decorations on the walls, I've picked them up, here there and everywhere, from auctions, to shipyards, to rummage sales, to garage sales. Anywhere I could find the stuff. I'm afraid, like father like daughter. He has passed his passion for the sea down to me."

"So you're a sailor?"

She laughed. "I wish. I just don't have the time. Or the boat. But on occasion, I do take your grandmother's boat out. I guess it's your boat now."

"There was a boat listed on the sheet Mr. Bissell gave me. I'm afraid I still haven't had time to absorb all of this. Money is something I've never had a lot of, or for that matter, never expected to have a lot of."

"Now that you're rich," Nicole smiled at him, "are you going to quit the police force?"

"Quit? I've thought about it over the years. There have been times," Bobby stared out the window, "that I wished I had done anything but be a cop." He turned and looked back at Nicole. "But I am a cop. Money or not, I guess I always will be a cop."

"You know," Nicole said, "You're grandmother was very proud of you.'

"I wasn't aware she even knew I existed!"

"Bobby, I don't want to get personal and I know it's none of my business, but she told me about your mother and your father. She had many regrets what happened."

Bobby's eyes turned cold. "She should have. They both should have!" He took a big gulp from his glass, emptying it.

"Let's not get into that. How did you meet them?"

Nicole picked up both of their glasses and walked back to the bar, talking as she went. "As I said, my father and uncle were both builders. Your grandfather called them for a remodeling job when your parents lived in Sterling, Illinois. That's when your grandfather and my father became very good friends. They played horseshoes and gin rummy together all the time. Your grandparents used to come over to our house frequently for dinner. Your grandmother loved the way I cooked. She used to tell me that when I was older she was going to set me up in a restaurant. She kept her word. Voila! Le Fleur."

"Who taught you to cook? You're mother?"

"No. I never knew my mother. She died giving birth to me."

"I'm sorry," Bobby interjected.

"I have no pain about it. I only knew her through my father's eyes and memories. He told me that I'm a lot like her." He hesitated for a moment, then turned to the table with fresh drinks for both of them. "Anyway I started cooking for my father when I was only 8 years old, and I've been cooking ever since. It's like therapy to me. Some people sew. Some paint. I cook. And when I'm angry," she looked at Bobby her eyes gleaming mischievously, I'll bake enough bread to feed your entire police department."

"So bread is a dead give away?" Bobby said grinning.

"A dead give away!" She responded. "Speaking of bread," she looked at her watch, "I usually have a midnight snack before I go home. Would you care to join me?"

"Just as long as you promise you won't start baking bread."

"Scouts honor," she said holding her hand over her heart. "Follow me."

The soft, plush carpeting absorbed the sound as they walked down the stairs and trough the restaurant. Brass and glass sconces equipped with solar sensors, softly lit their way. When they entered the huge, well equipped kitchen, the stainless steel fixtures were bathed in a hue of red from the armed burglary alarm that was perched high in the corner.

Nicole went to the main bank of switches and turned on the fluorescent light that lined the room. They both squinted as the room was engulfed in light. Nicole grabbed a white cook's apron and slipped it over her head.

"How about a Jimmy Sandwich?" She asked as she opened the cooler door.

"What in the hell is a Jimmy Sandwich? Is that one of your concoctions?"

"I wish. I could take the credit for it, but a very dear, sweet man from New Jersey made it his claim to fame. Do you like steak?"

"Sure. Who doesn't?"

"Trust me," she said as she emerged from the cooler with beef tenderloin in one hand and a tube of butter in the other. She set both items down on the butcher-block counter top that ran parallel to the stoves, grills and deep fat fryers. Then she walked over to the pantry and brought out a loaf of thinly sliced white bread and a gallon jug of Vigo Olive Oil. She put eight slices of bread in the two toasters and turned to light the stove. Hanging above the stoves were skillets, pots and pans of all sizes and shapes. After she chose the proper sized pan, she put it over the flame and poured in just enough olive oil to cover the bottom of the pan. Next, she skillfully cut four thin slices of tenderloin with a large butcher knife. When the toast popped up, she buttered each piece and then in one quick stroke, cut the crust from each side with the butcher knife. Bobby watched, fascinated. She worked as efficiently and smoothly as a well oiled machine, never missing a stroke. Bobby, who had skipped dinner, found that he was ravenously hungry all of a sudden.

"I hope you like your meat rare. It's the only way I make these."

"I never argue with a woman who is holding a butcher knife. Rare is fine, I like it rare!" Bobby replied, holding his hands back in a gesture of surrender.

The meat barely touched the oil before she turned it over. She removed the meat from the skillet just as quickly. Next she cut the four sandwiches in half and put two sandwiches on each of the gold-rimed, Limaoge dinner plates. She garnished each plate with a sweet green onion and a small piece of cantaloupe.

"Ready?" She asked. Not waiting for an answer she turned and walked through the kitchen doors and into the plaid dining room Bobby had seen earlier. She set the plates down at one of the window tables in the darkened dining room and lit the candle.

"Sit," she said. "I'll be right back."

"The light from the lone candle illuminated just the immediate area. The other table and chairs in the dining room were just silhouettes in the shadows. The stillness of the room was gently interrupted when Nicole turned on the background music, Frank Sinatra singing 'My Way.'

Nicole reappeared with a chilled bottle of wine of Perrier Jouet and two crystal champagne glasses. "I thought we should celebrate our new partnership, and I hope" she said looking directly into Bobby's eyes, "to a long and lasting relationship." The cork emitted a soft pop.

Nicole leaned close to Bobby as she poured the champagne into his glass. Their bodies touched slightly. Once again, he could smell her sweet and light scent, a scent of night blooming jasmines, swaying gently in a tropical breeze. He suddenly realized he was not hungry anymore. Bobby reached over and put his hand on top of Nicole's hand. He gently set the bottle that Nicole was holding, back down on the table. He put his other hand on her waist and slowly turned her face to him. He kissed her gently on the lips.

She pulled back, slightly. Again he pulled her close to him and kissed her gently. They looked at each other for a long moment. Then, with their hearts pounding, they kissed deeply, longingly, each responding to the other's touch as if they were one.

Bobby scooped her up in his arms and carried her out of the dining room and up the stairs to the lounge and the comfort of the soft sofas where they had started the evening. They both knew this was only the beginning.

CHAPTER 11

The loud, pulsating tone of the phone jarred Bobby from the deep sleep he was enjoying and brought him back to semi-consciousness. His hand automatically searched the end table, next to his bed, to find the source of the incessant and disturbing noise to stop it. Not being able to locate Ma Bell with his eyes closed, he rolled over on his side and opened his eyes in an effort to locate the misplaced instrument of chatter. The end table, not only did not have his phone on it, but it wasn't his end table. For that matter, he was not in his own bedroom. His mind quickly traced his recent past in an effort to pinpoint his present whereabouts. Then, he felt a movement beside him and heard a sleepy voice say, "Yes he is. Just a moment." Only then did he realize he was with Nicole. In her bed.

She rolled over to face him. An impish smile crossed her sleepy face. She handed him the phone. "Jiggers! I think it's the cops," she quipped.

Bobby smiled, kissed her lightly on the nose and took the phone. "Ya!" he answered.

"And just when I was beginning to think you were celibate," Coffee said, chuckling to himself.

Bobby could almost see the smirk on Coffee's face as he talked. "Coffee, cut the bull shit and just tell me why you called."

The clowning tone disappeared from Coffee's voice. "I think we've got another one."

Bobby sat straight up in bed. "Where?"

"The Pig Pen Bar and Grill, off Halstead and 42nd Streets, in the Whiskey Point area, next to the old amphitheater. One of the kids who works in the kitchen went out back to empty some trash. That's where she found the victim, or part of her anyway, hanging out of the dumpster. We found the rest of her stuffed in a bag that was thrown on the top of the trash.

"Is Walt there yet?"

"He got here just a few minutes ago."

"I'm on my way!" Bobby hung up the phone.

Nicole sensed the seriousness of the call and was now wide awake. She sat up in bed. "Can you tell me, or is it privileged information?" she asked as she watched Bobby get dressed.

"We think The Butcher has given us another victim. They found her in a trash dumpster. I've got to go."

"Oh! How terrible!" Nicole Shuddered. "I hope you nail the creep!"

"We're working on it," Bobby said as he headed for the stairs that descended to the living room below.

"Am I going to see you again?" The look in her eyes and the tone of her voice referred to the intimacy they had shared.

He walked back to the bed and sat down beside her. "Just try and keep me away." Then, holding her face gently in both hands, he kissed her deeply and passionately. He could feel the heat beginning to grow in his groins. Nicole felt it too. Gathering all of his restraint, he pulled back, but only because he knew he had to. "I'll call you later," h said and kissed her again, only more lightly this time. Then he got up and left.

The Pig Pen Bar and Grill had definitely seen better days. It was located in an area that had once boomed with business from the stockyard workers. When the stockyards closed in 1971, so did most of the other establishments in the area. Now, most of the buildings were boarded up. Only a few of the taverns had survived, due to the locals who frequented them. The Pig Pen Bar and Grill was one such establishment.

The inside of The Pig Pen Bar and Grill was even dingier than the paint-peeled sign outside led you to believe. Three worn, felt, pool tables and several sets of battered, wooden tables and chairs took up most of the floor space. A long L-shaped bar with backless, maroon, naugahyde and chrome bar stools with most of the seats ripped from abuse, took up the rest of the room. Stuffed pig's heads and shelves loaded with pigs of every shape and size decorated the wall space behind the bar. All were layered with dust.

Bobby noticed Coffee standing in front of the bathroom doors. One was marked BOARS and the other was marked SOWS. He was talking to a short, overweight man who wore a dingy, gray, sleeveless tee-shirt. A food, stained apron covered the man's protruding belly.

Bobby heard Coffee's voice rise as he said, "We'll get out of your hair as soon as we're done and not a minute before. So, unless you want me to charge you with obstructing justice, I suggest you sit down over there and stay out of the way. You got that?"

The man in the apron muttered some obscenities as he walked away form Coffee. He sat down angrily on one of the bar stools and hit the counter with his first.

"What's the problem?" Bobby asked as he approached Coffee.

"Dick Head here's the owner. He objects to our boys going over the place. Says he's got paying customers coming in shortly who get jittery in the presence of Chicago's finest."

If they're jittery, it's because they haven't had their morning fix!" Bobby said. "Now, where's the body?"

"Out back." Coffee said. "This way."

Bobby followed Coffee behind the bar and through a kitchen he couldn't imagine had ever passed the health board's inspection. They ended up in the alley behind The Pig Pen Bar and Grill. Several squad cars, along with the meat wagon, were lined up in the narrow alleyway. Walt was leaning against one of the cars, waiting for Bobby's arrival. As soon as he saw Bobby, he walked towards him, shaking his head.

"I'd lay money on it, Bobby, this is the same guy. Everything matches, right down to the wound on the back of the head. I'll have to check the impressions on the wound to be positive but I have a feeling it's just going to be routine."

Together, they walked over to the mutilated body that lay on the ground next to the dumpster.

"This body, just like the others, is almost devoid of fluid," Walt said. He picked up the green canvas bag. "Most of her body was stuffed in this."

"He probably pitched it into the dumpster. It will be a waste of time to look for prints. I'd say we've come to just another dead end, "Coffee said as he walked up to join them.

"All we've got dead, is a body!" Bobby growled as he looked down at the dismembered, naked woman. He turned his attention back to Walt and Coffee. "I think the killer has just given us our first lead."

"What lead?" Coffee asked, picking up the canvas bag. "An old sea bag?"

Bobby was about to answer him, when a voice behind him said, "Coffee, Coffee, Coffee." Kodak was shaking his head from side to side. "Not the sea bag, man. The location." Kodak walked up to Bobby and causally threw his arm over Bobby's shoulder. He had a big toothy grin on his face. The connection is Halstead Street."

"And would you enlighten Captain Anderson here. Tell him how you reached that conclusion. "Bobby said looking down Kodak.

"Elementary, my dear Watson. Elementary." Kodak replied, imitating the English dialect. He removed his arm from Bobby's shoulder and addressed both Walt and Coffee. A serious tone returned to his voice as he gazed down at the dead woman. "Number one, Jessica Ellis, disappeared only six blocks from here. Number two, this alley dead ends and is virtually inaccessible. Only someone who knows the area would know this alley was located here. I think our killer is close. He may have even grown up in the area."

"Kodak's right." Bobby said. "Coffee, concentrate your men in a two mile radius of the site. I want the entire area sealed off. If he's in the area, and I think he is, we're going to find him. "I don't' want any stone left unturned. Got it?"

"I'll get right on it," Coffee said.

"And Walt, get on that head wound as soon as you get back. Let's make sure this is the same killer. I don't want to end up with egg on my face."

"You've got it! I'll call you as soon as I'm done."

Bobby and Kodak watched Walt and Coffee walk in different directions as they both started to put the wheels in motion in their perspective divisions.

"Speaking of egg," Bobby said to Kodak, "I'm starved. Let's get some breakfast."

Kodak, who was still standing only a few feet from the mutilated corpse. Looked from the dead woman to Bobby and shook his head in amazement. "How you could eat, after seeing this is beyond me." Then smiling, he continued, "unless, of course, you've had the love of a good woman."

"I'll be damned," Bobby thought to himself. Coffee sure didn't waste any time spreading the word. By tonight, the news would probably be on the front page of the Police Gazette, or as his fellow officers called it, the P.P.P., for Police Peyton Place.

Mike hardy had started his morning without his partner, who had called sick with the flu. It seemed the entire Windy City had been besieged by an epidemic. His wife, Maggie, who was a nurse in the geriatric ward of the Michael Reese Hospital said that the hospital had been absolutely inedited with flu cases. It seemed this strain of flu was especially hard on the elderly.

Mike looked down at the sheet of paper he was holding. The paper listed buyers who had been present at the Argos Meat Plant auction. He had three business' names left to check out. The first, Maxwell Brother's, was located in Des Moines, Iowa. He had already booked the flight out of Midway for this evening. He was going to meet with Sam Maxwell, the one brother who had attended the auction, at 9:00 A.M. in the morning. The next name on the list was the Marino Fish Market which was located down on Water Street. The last name was Partridge & Son's Salvage Inc. which was located over on 35th Street, near Comisky Park.

It didn't really matter which one he went to first since he was probably an equal distance between the two.

Mike decided to save the Marino Fish Market for last since it was located on Water Street with all the other produce markets. Water Street was the best place in the city to pick up fresh fruits and vegetables, along with fresh fish and shell fish. Going there was like walking into another world. One was immediately confronted by the commotion of sellers and buyers alike, all waving their hands and raising their voices as they bartered over the cost of the goods. Sellers complained of the huge profits the sellers were making. Mike got a kick out walking from stand and haggling over everything form tomatoes to zucchini. He loved grocery shopping. In fact, grocery shopping was the only type of shopping he enjoyed. Maggie had done it during the early years of their marriage, sixteen years ago, but somewhere along the line Mike had taken over the responsibility and he loved it. So once a week, usually on Friday, armed with coupons clipped form Thursday's newspaper, Mike would make his way to his favorite grocer to pick up their weekly supply of food. He knew the butchers and most of he check-out girls on a first name basis.

Maggie always teased him. She said most men got a hard-on looking at Playboy Magazine. Mike, she said, got a hard-on from looking at corned beef cabbage. It wasn't true of course, he thought smiling to himself, but she wasn't far form the truth either. He was starting to get hungry just thinking about the grocery shopping. He'd have to make a point of looking for a nice head of sugar loaf cabbage while he was down at Water Street today. He made a right turn on 35th Street, looking for Partridge & Sons Salvage Inc. He found it with no trouble. It was in the middle of the block, jammed between Harper Scrap and Chicago Fastener Products Company.

Joe Partridge was a large, jovial man in his early fifties. He cleared a few cartons off a chair in his cluttered office so Mike could sit down.

"Mr. Partridge, I understand you were one of the buyers at the Argos Meat Packing Plant auction. We're investigating the murder of five women who were found in that building," Mike said.

"I figured that," Joe Partridge replied with a laugh. "Didn't figure you came all the way over here to buy some nuts and bolts from me. Sure, I was a buyer. I'm a buyer at almost every auction. Auctions are my bread and butter. How do you think I got started in this business? We buy and sell anything by the pound, piece, or penny." Joe Partridge leaned back in his swivel chair, put his hands behind his head and smiled with pride.

"What, exactly, did you purchase at the auction, Mr. Partridge?"

"Let me see," Partridge said. He got up from his desk and yelled into the adjoining office. "Kimmy, get me the bill of sale form the Argos auction."

Within a few minutes, a pert, young brunette brought the bill of sale into the office and laid it on the desk in front of her boss. "here you go Dad," she said and then quickly scampered out of the office.

"Here, see for yourself." Joe Partridge handed Mike the piece of paper.

"It says here, you purchased a 1973 Clark lift truck, a five hundred pound capacity scale, a wooden desk and a box of miscellaneous. Is that correct?"

"Sure is. The only thing I've got left is the lift truck. Kept that for myself. Sold the rest of the stuff before I even got out the door."

"What do you mean, Mr. Partridge? Before you got out of the door?"

"Ole John bought them off me. He buys everything. Reminds me of a pack rat. Never sells anything, just buys."

Mike sat straight up in his chair. "John who?" he asked.

"Can't say I really know his last name. He owns this place over on 55th Street and Garfield called Trash and Treasures. I see a lot of him at the auctions. Guess he travels the circuit too. He wanted the desk real bad. He paid me so much extra I felt guilty and threw in the box of junk I had bought. Never got a chance to even see what all was in it."

"Do you happen to have the receipt from that sale?"

Joe Partridge smiled with pride again as he got up and yelled, "Kimmy!"

Mike pulled his squad car up in front of Trash and Treasures. The huge, tin building was rusted from neglect. The sagging roof looked as if it were about to collapse. A large window with small panes, in the front of the dilapidated building displayed knick-knacks of every kind, shape and size. Bikes, wooden benches, and old gas pump, copper weather vanes, chairs and an assortment of odds and ends lined the front of the building. The front door was ajar. An 'OPEN' sign hung from the front of the door. Inside, the building was just as cluttered. It was as crowded with junk and furniture as a junk yard is with old cars and hub caps.

"Hello. Anybody here?" Mike called as he cautiously made his way through the maze of items that lined the floor. His right hand was tense and positioned to pull his weapon if necessary. The huge barn-like structure smelled musty. Particles of dust danced in the sunlight that streamed through the high perched windows in the back or f the building.

Mike walked along the L-shaped glass counter. It contained some old costume jewelry, silverware and other assortment of junk. He spotted a doorway, at the end of the counter that he figured must lead to another room. As he approached the doorway he said, "Anybody . . . ."

The movement of the sickle was just too quick and too unexpected to allow Mike any chance to respond. He never even saw the man who was hiding on the other side of the wall, only the hand on the handle of the sickle. The sharp, curved blade severed Mike's head from his body as easily as a knife cuts through warm butter. His head flew backwards, rolling from side to side on the wooden floor, leaving a trail of blood as it bounced from one side of the building to the other before it finally came to rest beside an antique milk pail. His body stood, headless, for at least three seconds, blood gushing in thick spots spurts from the neck before it finally fell forward and crashed into a stack of pots and pans that lay on the floor.

It was doubtful that Mike Hardy had felt anything. He never would again.

CHAPTER 12

John Beltzer looked down at Detective Mike Hardy's bleeding, headless body. A large pool of blood encircled Mike's shoulders. John rolled Mike over on his back and then searched Mike's pockets in an effort to locate the keys to the squad car parked out front. He removed the 38 Police Special from Mike's shoulder holster and put it in the back pocket of his own pants. Next, he found Mike's wallet, took the forty-seven dollars and then pitched the wallet.

He knew he had very little time. He walked over to the front door and turned the OPEN sign over so that it read CLOSED instead. He pulled the shade down, closed and locked the door, and then walked out to the street. He checked to make sure no one was watching before he got into Mike's unmarked police car, started the engine and drove it around the back of the building to the other storage shed on the property. He got out of the car and pushed the sliding double doors of the storage shed wide open and then drove inside.

He parked the patrol car beside the six other cars that were already parked inside. He had never expected to add a police car to his collection. All of a sudden the police radio crackled to life, startling him. He didn't know what a Code

15 was. It did make him very nervous though. Small beads of perspiration covered his forehead. His hands were slick with sweat.

Once back inside the main building, he went directly to Mike's body. He stared down at it and grinned as he said, "So you thought you were a big man. Huh, cop? Well you're not so big anymore, are ya? You prick!" He was screaming now. "Don't you know it's bad your health to hang around this neck of the city? Real bad! Ya know what I mean? Yeh, you shouldn't be hanging around this neighborhood!"

John Beltzer laughed. His jet black eyes glistened with excitement. A small stream of spittle ran from the corner of his mouth down his chin. It clung in gleaming drops to his short, wiry, black beard. He knelt beside Mike's body and started to undress it.

"Thought you had me, didn't you. Prick! Ha!" He laughed again as he removed Mike's jacket and shirt. "Joe Partridge let the cat out of the bag though. He called. You didn't expect him to call me. Did you? Told me you were coming. He was afraid I'd give you the true price of that desk he sold me. The cheap bastard! I knew you were coming." He lifted the shoulders of the headless man off the ground and talked to te air where the head should have been. "I knew!" he screamed. He laughed as he lowered the body back to the ground. As he removed the rest of Mike's clothing he softly sang to himself,

"If I knew you were coming, I'd baked a cake, baked a cake, baked a cake. If I knew you were coming, I'd baked a cake. How'd ya do. How'd ya do. How'd ya do."

When he completed the task, he dragged Mike's body to the back of the building where he frantically searched through the piles of boxes until he finally found the old block and tackle and the hay hook he was looking for. He tied the hay hook to the rope on one end of the block and tackle. There was a large steel hook in the exposed wooden beam above him. He liked to use it to display things he wanted people who walked into his store to see. Sometimes he used it for other things, like Ellen Parker. A wide grin covered his face as he recalled how her nude body had danced in the air.

"Ya, cop", he said as he buried the hay hook deep into Mike's naked back. "You just shouldn't of been hanging around this neighborhood." He attached the eye of the block and tackle to the hook in the low beam. Then he pulled, with all his might, on the other end of the rope. Slowly, Mike's body inched its way up into the air. Between grunts, Johnny said, "everybody's going to get good look at you cop. A real good look." He laughed. "Yup, you shouldn't of been hanging around here. Just ain't healthy!"

He continued to chuckle as he tied the rope. When he was finished, he stepped back to get a better look at his handy work. Shaking his head in approval, he walked back to get the missing head. His eyes searched the room for the perfect display perch as he stood beside the head. When they came to rest on the child size, metal wastebasket that was decorated with cartoon characters of Porky and Petunia pig, his eyes sparkled. "How fitting!" He exclaimed and clapped his hands together with child-like glee.

He retrieved the wastebasket and the head and then returned to the dangling body. He sat the wastebasket on the floor and carefully placed the head in it. It was a beautiful fit. A large toe on the back of one of the swinging feet, slightly brushed the soft, brown hair on the back of Mike's head as the body swung back and forth.

"And it's kick off time," Johnny sang as he watched the scene.

He whistled as he went into the room at the back of the building to shower and change. In less than half-hour he was ready to go. He walked through the building gathering his treasures. Trip by trip, he piled the stuff into the back of his pick-up truck. When he had finished he walked back inside and stood his hands on his hips as he looked around the building. With a final look at Mike Hardy's body, he turned, walked out the door, locked it, and got into the cab of his truck. "You might know who I am," he said, staring at the building, "but try and catch me. Catch me if you can," he taunted.

Inside the storage shed, the police radio dispatcher could be heard barking instructions, in code, to patrol cars everywhere in the district. But when the dispatcher was told, by Captain Anderson, to raise Detective Hardy on the radio, she couldn't.

Coffee thought that Mike had probably stopped to take his morning shit.

CHAPTER 13

B reakfast had been a disaster and the way things were going lunch probably wouldn't be any better. The first thing Bobby and Kodak saw before they entered the coffee shop, was the front page headlines of the Chicago Morning Sun.

'WOMEN ALIVE WHEN BUTCHERED. SUSPECT SOUGHT'.

Bobby pulled the paper out of the bright, yellow, metal dispenser with enough force to send it tottering. Only Kodak's quick reflexes kept it from falling over.

"That bitch!" Bobby growled through clenched teeth as he read the article. "How in the hell did she get this information? There's got to be a leak." He looked at Kodak. "And it's got to be on Walt's end. Come on!"

"What about breakfast?"

"Fuck breakfast! We'll grab some coffee at McDonald's. It's on the way."

"McDonald's again." Kodak said shrugging his shoulders. "I might have known."

"Where are we going?" Kodak asked as they pulled away from the curve.

"We're going to shove this paper up Jane Dwyer's ass! Any more questions?" Kodak knew by the tone of Bobby's voice that it was time for him to keep his thoughts to himself.

Bobby squealed to a stop in front of the Sun News building paying no attention to the 'Tow Away' signs that lined the street. He threw open the door and stomped through the revolving front doors. Kodak had to break into a run just to keep up with him. Bobby stormed past the receptionist as he stood in protest.

"Sir, can I help you? Sir wait!"

Bobby ignored her pleas and kept walking. The clamor of machines and people ceased as he made his way through the maze of desks in the newsroom. Papers flew from the rush of the wind his stride created. His eyes never left the plush glass enclosed office at the end of the room. Jane Dwyer was on the phone absorbed in conversation and completely unaware of Bobby's impending arrival. It wasn't until her door was thrown open with such force that it hit the wall behind it that she knew Bobby had arrived.

"You fucking bitch!" Bobby's voice was seething with rage. He threw the paper down on her desk.

"I'll call you back later." she said abruptly hanging up. "Well inspector Cash, as usual your vocabulary is as primitive as your manners."

"Where did you get this information?" Bobby demanded. He leaned down and glared directly into her eyes.

"I have my sources"

"I'll bet you do. When I find out who I'm going to nail their tongues to the wall!"

"Can I quote you inspector?" She smugly asked.

"Oh you can quote me. And quote this! If one more woman dies because of your unprofessional form of journalism, because of your complete lack of conscience, I'm going to be all over you like cheap perfume on a whore!"

Jane stood her gray eyes cold and piercing. "If it's not true, sue me! Otherwise get the fuck out of my office!"

They stared at each other. Hatred showed in both their eyes. Abruptly Bobby turned and left. Jane Dwyer watched him until he was completely out of sight. A smile of victory covered her face. "I'm going to castrate you you bastard!" She said as she slammed the door shut.

Kodak glanced at Bobby from time to time as they drove in silence to headquarters. Bobby's blue eyes stared at the highway in front of him. The taut skin beneath his pronounced cheekbones occasionally quivered from anger.

Kodak wasn't exactly sure why Jane Dwyer had a personal vendetta against Bobby. He only knew that it existed. Bobby never talked about it. For all the years he had known him he never heard Bobby talk about his personal life except of course to tease him about an occasional girlfriend. They shared almost every waking hour for the last two and a half years including many a rollicking night. But in all that time Kodak couldn't recall any serious conversations of a personal nature. Even the other night when they went out to dinner, after the lawyer in the expensive suit visited Bobby in his office he didn't say anything about it. He had only said that it wasn't important.

Bobby was respected and feared by many of his peers. He had the same effect when he entered a room full of police officers as an old spinster English teacher would have walking into a disruptive classroom. Often the laughter and conversation would cease as soon as he entered the room. But Kodak knew a different man, a kind man.

Kodak could remember when Bobby moved his Mama out of the ghetto and into a nice little house on the south side. Bobby bought her all new furniture, something most people in the ghetto only see in store windows or in television advertisements. She was so proud and happy of her new surroundings. She insisted that Bobby come for a celebration dinner.

Kodak would never forget that hot July morning when his senses were aroused, not by the aroma of frying bacon and eggs, but by the permeating fragrance of a twenty-three pound turkey roasting in the oven.

"Mama!" He exclaimed as he entered the cheerfully decorated kitchen. "What are you doing? It's not Thanksgiving."

"Oh, but it is!" She happily replied as she bustled around the kitchen. "Tonight we're giving thanks to the Lord," she hesitated, "and to Inspector Cash." She pointed a fragile finger in his direction and commanded, "and don't you be late!"

"We won't Mama. I promise." He said as he sat drinking his coffee, watching her, and sharing in her happiness. She was so small. She barely reached the center of Kodak's chest. Even though her fingers were knotted from arthritis and her face was cracked with age and hardship it was her strength and determination that got them all those lean bad years. He would make sure that she never suffered or wanted again.

That evening for the first time since they moved into the house they ate in the dining room. The table was set with the best dishes she had. The turkey had been cooked perfectly and was stuffed with cornbread dressing. The platter was decorated with brightly colored marigolds and zinnias his mama had cut from the garden. She proudly placed the platter in the center of the table. Side dishes of mashed potatoes and gravy, snap beans, candied yams, cranberries and homemade biscuits surrounded the platter of turkey.

She dressed in her finest Sunday dress and fussed when Bobby pulled out her chair to seat her. "Mercy!" She exclaimed, "All I need now is some of those fancy silver candlesticks and I'd feel like a grand lady."

"But you are a grand lady." Bobby said as he leaned down and kissed her lightly on the cheek. She giggled in deep pleasure.

"Thomas." She said. "Please say grace."

Dinner was delicious. They ate until they could barely move. She refused any assistance in the kitchen. "Cleaning up," she said, "is women's work." When she returned from the kitchen she surprised both Kodak and Bobby with a bottle of Hennesy brandy and two glasses.

"I hope you like this kind." She said. "The man at the liquor store said it was the best."

"It's my absolute favorite." Bobby replied.

Kodak's mother returned a large smile and then hurried back to the kitchen to finish her work.

"She's a piece of work." Kodak said. "She doesn't even approve of liquor."

"She sure is." Bobby said. "She sure is."

The next week Kodak's mama received a package from United Parcel Service. It contained a pair of silver candlesticks. The note inside read, "To a grand lady." The card was unsigned but she knew who sent the gift and so did Kodak. It was that kind of thoughtfulness that other people rarely saw in Bobby Cash.

"What are you smiling at?" Kodak heard Bobby asking.

"Oh, nothing. I was just thinking about Thanksgiving."

"Thanksgiving?" Bobby said shaking his head. "Kodak, sometimes I don't know about you."

Just as Kodak predicted the rest of the day went badly. The Police Commissioner summoned Bobby into his office and blamed him for the story in the morning paper. Walt confirmed that the woman they found was indeed the sixth victim of 'The Butcher'. The wound on the back of her head showed the same grill shaped pattern they found on the other five victims. To make matters worse during lunch they had the misfortune of catching the documentary on, 'The Chicago Butcher—A city in Fear'. The documentary was narrated by none other than Jane Dwyer. It was obvious to both Bobby and Kodak, as they watched her interview the owner of the Pig Pen Bar and Grill, that her source had to be inside the department. The discovery of victim number six had not yet been released to the press.

To say the least, Bobby's mood for the rest of the afternoon was grim. As the detectives checked in, one by one, at the end of their shifts it was also apparent by the expressions on their faces that their attempts to uncover leads came up empty.

Bobby had his feet propped up on the windowsill and was staring at the building across the street when Coffee entered his office.

"Archer and Higgins just checked in. They drew a blank on the list of buyers at the auction."

"What about Hardy and Townsend?" Bobby asked as he turned to face Coffee.

"Townsend called in sick this morning. Mike's supposed to be headed for Des Moines later today. He'd have called in if he had come up with anything. He probably didn't have any more luck than the rest of us."

Bobby glanced at his watch. It was 5:30 P. M. "Well, I'm calling it a day. If anything turns up, anything at all, call me."

Coffee nodded his head and silently retreated. Bobby noticed as Coffee walked away that his gait seemed to be slower than usual. His shoulders seemed more rounded. Age was beginning to take its toll. "I'll probably look like that in another twenty years." He thought to himself. The thought made him need a drink. He threw on his jacket and headed for the nearest bar.

Kodak had a bad feeling in his gut as he watched Bobby walk away. As long as he had been a cop and in almost every major murder case that he and Bobby had worked together on there had always been something that had turned the case around. Just one little slip of the tongue or one seemingly minor piece of evidence would eventually lead them to the killer. But somehow this killer managed to stay two jumps ahead of them. And with every two jumps they found another dead body. Another dead end so to speak. He felt as frustrated as Bobby and just as angry but instead of heading for a bar to vent out his frustrations he headed for ice cream and there was only one place in town, in his opinion, that could satisfy his fix. That was Wasserman's Confectionary Shop. It was probably the only thing Kodak missed about the old neighborhood growing up.

It was somewhat out of his way but worth the trip. He marveled at how Mr. Wasserman survived all those years in the ghetto. Not that it was that bad when Kodak was a little boy. There was still crime alright, but not like now. Now people killed for kicks not for needs. Most punks got high on booze not on drugs. Drugs fried the soul as well as the brain. It made life cheap and individuals even more dangerous.

Every Friday evening when he was a child he and his mama would walk down to Sid Wasserman's and have an ice cream cone. Just one dip that was all his mama could afford but a dip never the less and Mr. Wasserman used a big metal scoop. He would dip it into a container of water and then into his homemade buckets of ice cream. He watched the metal scoop slid through the creamy flavors and saliva would form in his mouth as he savored the taste before he even got his cone. No matter how many different flavors Mr. Wasserman made that day, Kodak always had the same. Chocolate. There was no other flavor for him.

He pulled his unmarked car in front of tattered building were Mr. Wasserman's shop was. The name on the glass was faded with age but could still be made out. The glare from the bright fluorescence overhead lights told Kodak the shop was still open. Kodak rubbed his ample stomach. He knew he didn't need the calories but the temptation was just too much. He turned off the car got out and walked into the shop. The old bell still tingled as he opened the door. Mr. Wasserman, who seemed ageless to Kodak stood behind the counter.

"Good evening Daniel." He said to Kodak lighting a cigarette as he talked. "How's that mama of yours?" He didn't let Kodak answer, but continued. "Pretty as ever, I suppose."

"Just fine. Mr. Wasserman. Just fine. I'll be telling her you asked about her. She'll be very pleased."

"Would you like your usual Daniel or has your taste broadened since your last visit?" He always asked the same question and Kodak always gave the same answer. It was kind of a game between them.

"The usual please and make it a quart instead of a pint." Kodak looked about the shop as he waited for his order to be filled. Nothing had really changed since he was a child. The small formica tables still gleamed in the light. The fake red brick linoleum pattern was worn thin in some places but still as clean as it always was. For Mr. Wasserman prided himself on his cleanliness. He would say when the health inspector paid him a call. "You can eat off the floor in my establishment or may God strike me dead!" You probably could, but Kodak didn't want to put it to the test.

"Here you go Daniel." He heard Mr. Wasserman say. That will be two dollars and eighty three cents. Kodak handed him three one dollar bills. He collected his change and ice cream said thank you and walked out the door. He got in his car waved at Mr. Wasserman who he could see standing behind the counter started his car and drove off.

But he didn't drive far. Just to the end of the block. Mr. Wasserman was in trouble. Something was wrong. Kodak knew that the minute the old man opened his mouth. In the first place he never smoked. His wife did and drove him crazy. He would scream at her in front of customers that it was unsanitary and he wouldn't have it in his store. In the second place he would ask about his mama but not once in all these years did he ever call her pretty and in the third place and most important of all he had given him strawberry ice cream.

He made his way around the block to the back of the store. He knew where the back entrance was and that the Wasserman's lived in the flat above the ice cream shop. When he reached the back of the shop he saw the main lights go out. He pulled out his gun and put his ear to the door. He could hear voices. Mr. Wasserman was one of them. He didn't know who the other was or if there was more than one. He heard a shriek and the sound of a body hitting the floor. His choices were very limited. He had to get inside and fast. He picked up the garbage can in the alley and ran around to the front. He threw the garbage can through the window. The glass shattered with a deafening crash. He heard a voice say, "What the hell was that!" and could make out the shadow of a figure moving towards the broken window. It gave him just the amount of time he needed to come through the back door.

"Police!" He shouted and was greeted by the blast of a gun. He could see the fire from its' muzzle and shot in its' direction. He heard a body fall collapsing against the broken glass. Kodak groped along the wall until his hand hit the light switches.

Beneath the glare on top of the once clean floor lay the motionless body of a young black male. Pieces of glass protruded from bleeding wounds. It was hard to tell which was made by a bullet.

He searched for Mr. Wasserman and found him unconscious in the store room. Looking at the gash in his head he could tell that he wasn't seriously hurt. He rushed up the steps to the apartment above to find Mrs. Wasserman bound and gagged on the living room floor. He untied her assured her that her husband was alright and called for assistance and an ambulance.

When Kodak came back down stairs Mr. Wasserman was standing up holding his head. "Daniel it's a good thing you only like chocolate." He smiled gratefully. "Now let me get you some on the house."

"No thanks Mr. Wasserman." Kodak said looking at the bloody mess on the floor. "I seem to have lost my appetite." Maybe he would stop at a bar and have a drink after all.

CHAPTER 14

There were eight keys on the key ring that Howard Bissell gave Bobby for the buildings on the estate. It took six tries before he finally found the right one. The lock on the front of his grandmother's house finally clicked open and allowed him to enter the dimly lit foyer. Even in the low lighting he could tell that fresh cut gladiolus had been placed in the crystal vase he noticed the other day. He wondered if Nicole had put them there.

He flipped the wall switches one by one until the brass and glass chandelier that hung above the table sprung to life. Although Nicole had taken him on a tour of the grounds he hadn't had enough time to explore the interior of the house, except for the library where he and Bissell had conducted their business. He remembered the well stocked bar in the library and decided to make himself a drink before embarking on his tour.

He had not intended to come straight here from headquarters. It had just happened. He was glad he was here now though. The peace and quiet of the house was more relaxing than a barstool at The Sign of The Trader where he usually stopped for a drink on his way home.

He took the bottle of Chivas from one of the mirrored shelves that lined the cabinet then picked up one of the extra large old-fashioned glasses and filled it until it was two-thirds full. The silver ice bucket that sat on the counter was empty. A little investigation revealed a pull out Scottsman behind the double doors beneath the counter. When he opened it he discovered that it was brimming with small square crystal-clear ice cubes. He scooped enough of the ice cubes into his glass to bring the amber colored liquid to the top of the rim. He took a large swallow so that he could walk about without spilling it. Now he would began his tour of the house.

The living room which was located on the other side of the foyer and it was larger than Bobby's entire downtown apartment. It was shaped like three sides of a rectangle. A white Yamaha Baby grand piano sat in the room's corner. A basket of purple iris were placed where a candelabrum might normally be located. One wall was made entirely of white brick including the fireplace. The longer wall at the back of the room overlooked the pool and patio. The french doors on this wall along with the twelve foot ceilings gave the room an open and airy look. The traditional style furniture were covered with either prints or solid colored fabrics in combinations of light sunny yellow or subtle cornflower blue. The furniture graciously surrounded the piano and fireplace.

The rays from the setting sun peeked through the woods at the back of the property and gave the room a warm mellow glow since there were no drapes or curtains on the high French doors. Though the color scheme he felt was feminine the comfortable feeling the room emitted would have made even the most macho of men feel at ease.

The remaining wall contained a complete entertainment center which held everything from a state of the art stereo system to a twenty-five inch built-in television. While exploring the shelf behind the doors of the center he found a fine collection of records mostly from the big band era. He looked through the records and selected one from, 'The Tribute to The Mills Brother's' album.

Satin Doll, one of Bobby's favorite song burst to life from speakers that were hidden from view. As Bobby walked out onto the patio he discovered that speakers, shaped like rocks, had been hidden among the superbly land escaped deck around the pool. He lingered momentarily as the sun flickered from sight before he walked back into the house.

The dining room,located off the living room, could comfortably seat twelve for dinner. A long mahogany table gleamed from lemon oil and the tender loving care it had obviously received over the years. The break front and hutch were filled with enough silver and china to give any cat burglar palpitations.

No expense had been spared in the kitchen either from the dark warm wood cabinets and delft blue tilled countertops to the matching double door sub-zero refrigerator and freezer. Bright cooper pots and pans hung from an oval wrought iron rack above the cobalt blue tilled preparation center. The center includes a breakfast bar with three bench wood stools. Bobby wondered if his grandparents had eaten their breakfast in here casually, or if they had dined at the long dining room table, her at one end and him at the other, both gazing out over the grounds of their amassed estate.

He opened the refrigerator expecting to find it empty. Instead he was surprised to find a lazy susan type tray covered in saran wrap and filled with cold cuts and cheese along with six bottles of Michelob, a loaf of rye bread, pickles, mayonnaise, mustard, a head of lettuce and last but not least a small round white vasefilled with flowers. A note taped to the vase read, "Sooner or later you have to eat". Signed "Nickel"

Bobby smiled to himself and made a gigantic sandwich. He passed on the beer and instead returned to the library to refresh his drink before he sat down to eat.

The Mills Brother's sang 'You're nobody till Somebody Loves You' and 'Tiger Rag' before he finished his meal. "This is the life." He thought to himself. He put the plate he used in the sink and watched the light of the moon reflect off the shimmering pool water from the kitchen window. He wondered how everything could look so deceptively beautiful here and be so brutally ugly in the city. He turned and walked up the flight of service stairs that led to the bedrooms above.

The first bedroom he came to was strictly a woman's room, probably his grandmother's. A bedspread of large pink roses covered the white four-poster bed. The walls and the carpet were the same shade of pink as were the sheer priscilla curtains and upholstered cushions that encased the massive bay window. He felt more like a peeping tom invading someone's privacy than the detective he was as he opened draws and cabinets to looking through his grandmother's personal effects. A hand carved rosewood chest that sat on her dressing table contained an exquisite collection of jewelry. Although he was no expert he had the feeling he was looking at a small fortune in jewelry.

The room across the hall he guessed must have belonged to his grandfather. The furniture was dark and heavy. Some of the walls were paneled in an equally dark wood. The carpet was a bold blue color. Two winged-back chairs, covered in a blue tartan plaid, matched the bedspread and sat in front of the built in fireplace. He stared at the painting on the wall above the fireplace. He switched on the small brass light that was located above it in order to get a better look. It was a painting of his mother and him when he was about five years old.

He had the original photograph from which the painting must have been copied. It had been taken in Grant's Park. His mother who at the time was in her early twenties, and perhaps the most beautiful woman he had ever seen, had been helping Bobby, who was chubby and tow-headed in the picture, get a drink of water from one of the park's many bubbling fountains. A passing photographer had snapped the picture. The next day the picture along with an article on Grant Park had appeared in the Chicago Tribune. It was undoubtedly Bobby's favorite picture of his mother. He gulped down the rest of his drink and considered going back down to the library for a refill. Then he spotted the three crystal decanters that sat on the small round table by the window. He knew he wouldn't have to go back downstairs. Instead he walked over to the table found the right bottle refilled his glass and sat down in one of the winged back chairs.

He stared up at the portrait of his mother and was soon filled with renewed hatred for his grandparents. Hatred he could never forget. He had only been five years old when he and his mother had stayed with his them on the farm in Sterling while his father was out at sea. One night, while he was sleeping, he'd been startled awake by his mother's screams. "Bobby!" she screamed. "Help me! Bobby, help me!" He had raced from his bed following the direction of her screams until he found her in the front room. His grandfather had tied her to a chair. She was twisting and turningscreaming Bobby's name, begging for help. He remembered yelling, "I'm coming mommy. I'm coming!" As he ran to her. His little hands grabbed at the ropes that bound her. Tears streamed down his face while he frantically tried to help her. Then his grandmother grabbed him and swooped him up out of his mother's reach. He clawed had her beating her with his fists. "Let me go! Let me go!" He cried. Even though he had know he was struggling to no avail he couldn't stop. He was sobbing fighting for his mother's life. But he was too little. He couldn't help her.

The next thing he knew two men both in white coats entered the room. They were carrying a stretcher. His grandfather untied the ropes that bound his mother while the two men held her down. She was screaming. They forced her arms into a white jacket with long sleeves and straps to bind her. Then one of the men picked up the black bag he had brought in with him. From the bag he pulled out a hypodermic syringe. Bobby couldn't take his eyes off of the long, gleaming needle. He was sure they were going to do something terrible to his mother. When they pulled her dress up on one side and jammed the needle into her thigh he nearly collapsed from fear. Then they took her away.

It was almost a year before Bobby saw her again. He never forgave his grandparents. From that day forward he had done everything he could think of to make their lives miserable. He had lived with them for another two years and had hated every moment of it.

It wasn't until he was much older that he learned the truth about his mother. His father finally told him that his mother was schizophrenic and had had the symptoms since she was a little girl. When his father married her, she was eighteen years old. Her parents never told his father anything about her disruptive behavior. Instead, they happily transferred their burden to him. They were relieved to be rid of her.

As the years went by, she had gotten progressively worse. The struggle to keep his job and some semblance of family life for the three of them was, at times, more than Bobby or his father could handle. His mother was in and out of mental hospitals, sometimes costing more a month than his father earned. When she was home, she was incapable, most of the time, of performing even the simplest of tasks, such as cleaning the house or preparing a meal. She would cause scenes anywhere and at any time.

Bobby learned at an early age that he couldn't bring his friends home since his mother would sometimes scream obscenities at them, throw things, or run into the front yard half naked to yell at invisible adversaries about imaginary grievances. Bobby would leave the house, sometimes not coming home for days on end in order to avoid the embarrassment he suffered because of her actions. Since his father was on the Great Lakes nine months out of the year, Bobby was able to come and go as he pleased most of the time.

Bobby's grandparents never offered assistance of any kind.

When his father died at sea, the responsibility of taking care of his mother came to rest entirely on his shoulders. He hated his father for leaving him and he hated his mother for making their life a living hell, even if it wasn't really her fault.

When his mother finally got so bad that she could no longer be trusted alone, Bobby had finally had to admit her to a mental hospital. She died there three years later. Now, he missed both his mother and father and regretted the fact that he had not had more time with them. If he'd only been older. If he'd only been wiser. If! If! If! It was too late now.

Bobby could feel the hot tears streaming down his face. "Too much booze makes you weepy," he said to himself. But he knew it wasn't the booze. He looked at his glass. The ice had melted. It was time for another. He went back down to the library. He'd seen enough.

Nicole found him sound asleep on the sofa in the library. His long, lean legs dangled uncomfortably over the arm of the chair. His sandy brown hair, cut boyishly short, hung in soft wisps across his forehead. Deep lines spread like tree branches from the corner of his eyes. Somehow, Nicole knew the lines were not from joy or sorrow, but from the intense concentration his job demanded of him. His dark, almost black, eyebrows and long lashes looked unnaturally out of place in comparison to his sandy colored hair, as if they belonged to someone of darker or more olive complexion. That, along with his straight, narrow nose and his cleft chin, gave him a ruggedly handsome appearance. Nicole smiled to herself as she sat down in the leather chair opposite him. His mode of dress was conservatively unfashionable and did nothing to enhance his tall, well-developed physique. He dressed more like Dirty Harry than Don Johnson. "One of these days," she thought, "I will have to take him shopping." She had a feeling that it wasn't going to be an easy task.

Bobby had taken the phone from the desk and had placed it on the coffee table next to him. His glass was nearly empty. He held it loosely in his hand which now lay on the floor next to the sofa. The empty glass explained to Nicole why Bobby hadn't answered her knocks at the back door. He looked so uncomfortable, her first instinct was to wake him up and send him off to bed just as a mother would send her child to bed. On second thought, however, she decided that he probably needed the sleep. It would be better to risk the chance of his waking up with a stiff neck and some cramped muscles and allow him to get what was probably some well needed sleep.

Nicole gently lifted the glass from his hand and placed it on the coffee table. Then she went to the linen closet, next to the downstairs powder room, to remove a thermal blanket and a bed pillow. She carefully eased the pillow under Bobby's head and covered him as best she could with the blanket. As she leaned down to kiss him on the forehead, she felt his strong arms encircle her, pulling her forcibly down on his chest.

"Now I know what they mean by the long arm of the law'."

She smiled as she looked into his dark, blue eyes.

"Just taking you into protective custody, ma'am," he replied, mimicking Joe Friday of Dragnet. "Just after the hard facts, ma'am. The hard facts."

They kissed. First as friends. Then as lovers, not stopping until they had to catch their breath.

"Speaking of hard facts," Nicole said as her fingers playfully explored the length of Bobby's body, finally coming to rest, gently but firmly, on his closed but bulging pants zipper, "How about a little undercover work?"

"I never thought you'd ask ma'am. I never thought you'd ask"

CHAPTER 15

J ohnny Beltzer poured another drink from the half-empty Jack Daniels bottle that sat on the wobbly formica kitchen table in front of him. He leaned back in the tattered, gray, vinyl covered chair and propped his feet up on one of the other chairs. The electricity had been disconnected for sometime in the deserted old farm house. He had to use the glass kerosene lanterns, he had found in the cellar, for light. He didn't mind not having electricity. In fact, he preferred the soft flickering glow the lanterns emitted over the harsh brightness of an overhead bulb.

In one hand, he held the front page of 'The Morning Sun'.

He sipped the undiluted bourbon from the jelly glass he had found in one of the cabinets. The reflection of the flame sparkled in his cold, black eyes. His lips were curled in a smug smile as he continually nodded his head as if he were giving constant approval to the article he was reading.

When he was finished reading, he set the paper down and raised his glass high in the air in a toast. "Here's to you Jane Dwyer, you blabbering bitch!" He gulped down the remainder of the bourbon and then refilled his glass. "So!" he said, talking to the shadows that filled the empty room. "You think you might know what I look like, huh?" He laughed. "Well, not anymore," he said, rubbing his cleanly shaved face. "What beard? I don't have a beard!" His face beamed with pleasure. "Look!" he said staring at the picture of Jane Dwyer that was displayed prominently beneath her '*by* line'. "I don't even have any hair on my head!" He ran both of his hands over the top of his newly bald head, laughing as he did.

Then suddenly, he became silent. His body became rigid. The expression on his face contorted with hatred. Viciously, he grabbed the newspaper and crushed it until it fit easily in his large, powerful hands. Jane Dwyer's picture loomed from the center of the crumpled mass. "I'll pay you back for this, you whore! I'll get you. I'll get you just like I got them all. You'll pay!" he screamed. "You'll pay!"

CHAPTER 16

It was the kind of day that had earned Chicago the nickname of The Windy City. A cold front from Canada had swooped down over the city, bringing high winds and dropping the late spring temperature from the comfortable seventies to more of a March-like fifty degrees. The sky was a depressing dark gray color and the cloud formations resembled those of a mid-winter snow storm as they intermittently doused the city with pelting rain and ice.

Bobby found it hard to concentrate on police matters even though Coffee was standing before him telling him that a woman from South Shore Plaza had identified Sharon Miles as one of the young women who had rented a booth from her at their annual arts and crafts show last April. That fact placed Sharon in the Halstead area at the approximate time of her disappearance and reaffirmed Bobby's hunch that their search had been concentrated in the right area. He knew the killer was out there, somewhere. It would just be a matter of time and a little luck on their part to smoke him out. The patrols were doing the best they could. Two square miles of buildings and people were a lot to cover. It was just a matter of time, but it was still a very slow and monotonous process.

Bobby was experiencing feelings he had never known before. He had always been very careful in his relationships with women to avoid any serious involvement. He had found out, at a young age, that his mother's illness could be hereditary so he had vowed he would never take the chance of allowing another human being to suffer as she had. That meant marriage and children were out of the question.

He and Patti Jacobs had had a good relationship until she brought up the topic of commitment. Then, just as quickly as a cell door slams shut to lock in its capture, an invisible wall had formed around Bobby. He had locked in his emotions and he had locked Patti out.

He had realized that with her background in psychology, it would have been easy to explain the situation to her, but the words just wouldn't come out. So instead, he had gradually become inaccessible, always busy when she called or with a slight distance in his voice whenever they spoke. Eventually they had faded apart. He always felt a bit awkward now when they were accidentally thrown together. The last time he'd seen her, she had told him she was dating some lawyer and that they were getting pretty close. Bobby was happy for her, although he sometimes felt a pang of regret when he looked into her warm, twinkling, green eyes.

But now there was Nickel. The wall that had always guarded his heart was crumbling. Last night, for the first time in his life, he had wanted to fulfill another person, not just be fulfilled. Although he had always considered himself a considerate lover, his patience would ultimately wear thin and his actions would be directed selfishly towards fulfillment of his own desires. But last night, as he and Nickel had lain intertwined, their naked bodies beaded with salty sweat, he had given no thought to his own needs, only to her's. He recalled, in slow motion, her body writhing with pleasure as he ardently pursued his only purpose—to give her all he had—to peek the sexual darkness in her until it screamed for light, until it pleaded to escape deep from within her. He needed nothing else, just that. He had made love to her. Consumed her. Then she had become the aggressor, the giver, loving him like no other woman had before. His body had begged. It had ached as it never had before as he prayed their love making would never end. And when it did, every fiber in his being exploded in unison, draining him of all will and reason and filling him with contentment and joy.

They had held each other close for a long time before they finally fell asleep. Each had been lost in their own private revelation. They were one now. They were in love.

Bobby was shaking his head, still trying to grasp the enormity of his feelings. A million things were racing through his head when the phone on his desk brought him back to reality.

"Inspector Cash?"

"Yes."

"Inspector Cash, this is Maggie Hardy."

"Yes Maggie, what can I do for you?" Bobby asked.

"Inspector Cash, I'm worried," Maggie said. The tone of her voice backed her remark.

"Why Maggie? What's the matter?" Bobby knew her well enough to know that she wouldn't call him unless she felt justified in doing so.

"Mike's disappeared! I can't find him anywhere!"

"But Maggie, he flew to Des Moines last night."

She interrupted him. "I know that! I packed his bag yesterday morning. But he told me he'd meet me a 1:00 P.M. for lunch at Shannon's Pub by the airport. He said his flight was due in at 11:45 A.M. I waited but he never showed up. He's never done that before!"

Bobby glanced at his watch. It was almost 3:00 P.M. "Maybe his flight was delayed Maggie. You know O'Hara field."

Again she interrupted him. "No, I checked. It left on time. I called the motel where he was supposed to be last night. He never checked in." She was close to tears. "I know something's happened!"

"Calm down Maggie. Where are you?" An alarm went off in Bobby's head, but he didn't want her to sense it.

"I'm at home now. I'm just . . . ."

"Listen Maggie. Stay there, just in case Mike tries to get in touch with you. I'll get right on it and as soon as I know something, I'll get right back to you. OK?"

"OK." Her response was barely audible.

"Hey Maggie," Bobby said with the most cheerful tone he could muster, "you keep that strong Irish chin up. It's probably just some kind of mix-up."

She had already hung up.

Cop's wives seemed to have a sixth sense when it came to the men in their lives. He hoped Maggie's instinct was wrong.

The next couple of hours were frantic. It was confirmed that Mike hadn't left Chicago for Des Moines like he had intended to. His partner, Townsend, who was still laid up with the flu, told Bobby and Coffee that there had been three names left on the list for them to check out, but since Mike had the list, he couldn't remember who they were. That meant Bobby had to locate the original list. At least they knew the Maxwell Brothers of Des Moines was one of the three remaining names. With any luck, the last two names would be listed along with them.

Detectives were required to check in and out daily but sometimes they didn't follow the rules. Whether from circumstance or just a lapse in procedure, it had been assumed that Mike had gone directly from his investigation to the airport. Bobby hoped it wasn't a fatal assumption on their part.

The process of elimination, along with Townsend's help, even as sick as he was, paid off. It wasn't going to be easy. It was Friday and after 5:00 P.M. so most of the city's business' had already shut down for the weekend.

"Rogers and I will check out the Marino Fish Market," Coffee said as he handed Bobby the last two names on the list. "You and Kodak take Partridge and Sons Salvage Company. Should we take back Up?"

"Let's just send out a couple of patrols in the immediate area. If Mike's in trouble, the sight of back-up could make it worse for him. We'll play it by ear."

The front doors of Partridge and Sons were locked. No sign of life could be seen from the offices behind the doors. Bobby motioned for Kodak to take one side of the long metal building.

Slowly, with guns drawn, they made their way to the loading docks at the rear of the building. They were just about to make their way up the adjoining concrete stairs when the rear entrance door swung open. A lanky, young man with curly, blond hair and a bad case of acne stepped out onto the loading dock.

"Freeze!" Kodak said, swinging into full view of the unsuspecting youth.

"Jesus!" the boy exclaimed, dropping the box and extending his arms up high over his head. "What's going on? I didn't do nothing!"

"Who are you and what are you doing here?" Bobby asked as he joined Kodak.

"My name is Jeremy Young and I work here. I was just closing up shop. See . . ." He started to reach for his wallet.

"Just a minute." Kodak said as he walked up the stairs and carefully approached the suspect. "I'll get that." Kodak took the young man's wallet at the same time he searched him. "He's clean Bobby. The I.D. fits. He's got a payroll check that's a match. "They withdrew their weapons.

"Who owns this place Jeremy?" Bobby asked.

"Mr. and Mrs. Joe Partridge." Jeremy said with a sigh of relief.

"Where can we find them?"

"Well, I know they live in La Grange somewhere, but they won't be there, at least not tonight."

"And why's that?" Bobby asked.

"Because it's the weekend and every weekend they go up to their cottage at Power's Lake in Wisconsin." He smiled proud of his knowledge. "They left about thirty minutes ago."

"OK Jeremy, you can lock up and go now. You've been a big help."

They watched Jeremy quickly close and lock the door, retrieve his box and then scramble away in his Bronco.

"Now what?" asked Kodak.

"Let's check with Coffee and see what he's got. If he doesn't have anything, we'll just have to wait until we can reach the Partridge's at Power's Lake."

Another two hours passed before Bobby was finally able to reach the Partridge's on the phone. Joe Partridge relayed the conversation he and Detective Hardy had had the day before.

"I finally sent him over to John's place on 55th and Garfield. A place called Trash and Treasures."

"Mr. Partridge, would you describe John for me, please?" Bobby asked.

Well, he's kind of stocky and about 5'10". He's in his late thirties. He has jet black hair, and, oh yes, a bushy black beard."

"Shit! Bobby said, hanging up before Partridge could hear.

He knew Mike was in big trouble.

Squad cars came from everywhere to silently surround Trash and Treasures. Officers were quietly given instructions along with the positions they were to maintain. They anxiously prepared themselves for the worst. A check on the Trash and Treasures business license identified the owner as John Beltzer. A check with the Motor Vehicles Department supplied not only the type of vehicle he owned, a 1973 blue Ford pick-up, but also a recent photo of him. Kodak identified him as the same guy he had seen at the Argos Meat Packing Plant. Bobby held little hope that Mike was still alive.

Coffee gave the first signal. The lights on every squad car sprang to life. The rusty hulk of the building loomed forbiddingly in front of them as it was bathed in the harsh brightness of headlights.

"John Beltzer, this is the police. Come out with your hands up." Coffee's voice bellowed over the hand-held loudspeaker.

Only the emptiness of silence hung in the crisp, evening air.

"Come out with your hands up!" Coffee repeated his demand. Again there was no response. The armed officers, frozen combatively, held their breath. Bobby nodded at Coffee. Almost simultaneously, four heavily armed men, two at the front door and two at the rear, kicked open the doors, preparing themselves for combat. The officers behind them scrambled for cover, scattering among the saleable debris.

The artificial light only penetrated the perimeter of the gloomy interior of the building. Trained eyes searched for movement. It was Officer Marty Falcone who first spotted the dangling human form.

"Dear Mother of God!" he said making the sign of the cross. Detective Mike Hardy wasn't missing anymore.

CHAPTER 17

T he docks at Belmont Harbor were bustling with activity of weekend sailors. Bobby sat on one of the wooden benches that lined the seawall overlooking the piers and watched the boats being teaked, sails were being raised and motors sputtered to life. There was a parade of men, women and children carrying baskets and coolers filled with every imaginable food and drink boarding their vessels for a day of fun in the sun.

The weather had fully cooperated. The sun's rays shone brightly, unhindered in a nearly cloudless sky. Gentle swells gave the sparkling blue water a mirror-like calm, and a light but steady breeze filled the colorful spinnakers that were raised as the fleet of sailboats cleared the harbor entrance.

Though no verbal arrangement had been made, since none was needed, Nicole, or Nick, as he preferred to call her, and he had been living together in the main house of the estate ever since that night they had silently proclaimed their love for each other. She had redecorated one of the spare upstairs bedrooms to suit both of their tastes. Little by little their clothes began to fill the empty closets of the room just as their love began to to fill the empty spaces of their hearts.

They both agreed that they each needed a well deserved break and that a restful day on the water was just what the doctor ordered. Bobby arrived about an hour earlier than their scheduled meeting time, anxiously anticipating a relaxing day at sea.

As he sat staring at the captivating panoramic view, he reminisced about the past week. It had been a long week. All of Chicago mourned Mike Hardy's indignant death. Bobby insisted that Maggie not be put through the ordeal of identifying the distorted remains of Mike's body. He personally signed the coroner's release papers.

The funeral had been especially hard on everyone as they imagined the brutality the gentle man must have endured. Mike now lay beneath the lid of the cold gray steel casket. Maggie held up extremely well. It was only after the services at the grave site, as the mourners were walking away that she fell to her knees and weep openly for the first time that day.

They escorted her to the long black limousine when she turned to Bobby, her eyes brimming with unshed tears and said, "find this animal for me. For Mike. His soul will never rest until this man is punished for the degradations he committed!"

Bobby promised they would get him. He silently hoped he would be able to keep that promise.

It was obvious that John Beltzer had made a clean get away eluding the potential captors that planned to ensnare him. He did however leave some valuable information behind. The other cars that were discovered in the storage shed, along with Mike's patrol car, revealed the identities of the two unknown victims. One was Betty Baker, a nineteen year old run away from Fort Myers, Florida. She had been running away and involved with drugs since she was fourteen years old. Since her parents had been through this before they had not filed a missing persons report on her.

Bobby learned that when they were told of her death they had said they weren't at all surprised she had ended up that way and that maybe now they could get a good night's sleep. It seemed like a cold and callous remark for the parents of a butchered and molested daughter to make but Bobby had seen what kids were capable of doing to their parents. The jails were full of such kids. Last year Bobby and Kodak arrested a twelve year old boy on a drug related homicide. The kid had had $4500.00 cash in his pockets and ice water in his veins. He met with both of the kid's parents. They were good, decent, middle income type people and their son was making their life a living hell. It was hard to figure what had happened. Well Betty Baker's parent's living hell was over now. So was hers.

The other victim was identified as Ellen Parker, owner of a late model white Buick station wagon which parked in the shed with the rest of the cars. Blood stains found on the bathroom floor and splattered on the walls matched her blood type. Coffee and Bobby figured that she had been killed there and left to bleed to death. They figured Beltzer had then disposed of her body by pitching it into the trash dumpster behind the Pig Pen Bar and Grill which turned out to be less than a mile away. Her family, on the other hand, was devastated by her death.

The shed also contained a shallow grave. The body remains, a skeleton that had been found in the grave, were taken to the morgue for study. So far the only thing that Walt had come up with was that it had been the body of a man in his sixties or seventies and that the skull had been fractured. The body had been in the ground a long time and couldn't really be tied to John Beltzer yet.

The back two rooms of the main building had been used by John Beltzer as his living quarters. Walls constructed of unfinished plasterboard separated the bedroom from the rest of the building. Weathered wooden four by eight plank walls ran the entire length of the building and covered the floor. A soiled bare mattress rested on a battered and scarred early American maple bed frame and a matching dresser with missing drawers and handles were the only pieces of furniture in the room. A gray wool blanket and two uncovered pillows had been thrown in a heap next to the bed along with several articles of men's clothing, presumed to belong to Beltzer.

Picture frames made of various woods and metals in all sizes were displayed on top of the dresser. Most of the pictures were of the same woman. The pictures had been taken in the 1950's or 1960's judging from the style of dress. In some of the photographs the woman was alone and in others she was with a young child. A larger picture hung on the wall behind the dresser and depicted a scene, apparently taken at the Stock Yards, with three men posing byside a slaughtered gutted hanging steer, as if they were big game hunters displaying their hard fought trophy. John Beltzer was one of the men in the photograph.

It took a team of investigators four days to find anyone who had been associated with the Stock Yards who could remember John Beltzer. Elmer 'Hammer' Johnson a towering black man in his mid sixties remembered him well. They found Elmer living with his daughter and grandchildren in a crowded three bedroom apartment on the south side. Because of the racquet made by the grandchildren and the lack of privacy Bobby and Kodak took him to a local coffee shop where they could talk in relative peace.

"Yes sir, I remember little Johnny well enough. Haven't seen him since 1971 though. Not since the yards shut down.

"Tell us about him Mr. Johnson. Anything you can think of." Kodak said. He knew the old man would respond better to a black man's questions than he would to a white man's questions. Bobby sat silently sipping his cup of coffee while Kodak asked the questions.

"Oh, no need to call me Mr. Johnson!" He laughed exposing the glittering gold tooth at the front of his mouth. Everyone calls me Hammer. Been called Hammer since I was a young man. Got the name working in the yards. Worked in the yards most of my life. Since I was no more than a boy. I'd do anything they'd let me do for money. Shoveled shit. Whatever. Then when I was about twenty one of the men who killed the cattle don't show up for work. The boss he looks around and sees that I'm the biggest and strongest and tells me to do the job. Well in those days there weren't no fancy automatic guns to knock out those big heifers. I used only a sledge hammer to hit them square between the eyes. If you don't hit them just right you'd have to hit them a couple of times and it was kind of sad seeing them dumb animals stagger and fall and try to get up again. Well I took hold of that sledge hammer and looked that first dumb beast straight in the eyes. I raised that hammer high over my head and came down with all my strength. Killed him deader than a doornail, and everyone after that. Never missed! That's why people started calling me Hammer. Made me right proud too."

"That's amazing," Kodak said. "I can see why you'd be proud. But what about John Beltzer? Where'd you meet him and what was he like?"

"He was about fifteen years old when I first met him. He worked on the kill floor with me. After I'd kill them animals chains would be tied around their back legs and they'd be lifted into the air and moved down a track. Johnny's job was to slit their throats as they came past him. He liked that job too. Shit, we'd be ankle deep in hot sticky blood and he'd be smiling. Said once he'd almost get a hard-on slicing the jugular and watching the blood come spurting out. Never said much. Just did his job."

Bobby and Kodak glanced at each other.

"Did he have any family that you knew of?"

"His mama. Everybody knew his mama. Every payday she'd be waiting for him when we came out of the yards, her breasts hanging out of low-cut, brightly colored dresses. Her face all painted up like some two-bit whore. Guess she was too. Everyone said she'd do what ever you wanted her to do to you for a couple of bucks. Saw her sucking cock myself once on one of the drivers. You could tell Johnny hated it when she came flittering around to hang on the men. Can't say as I blamed him. She was a cunt! She'd take just about everything he made. Just leave him enough for one nights drinking. And drink he did. Get real drunk. Get mean too. Real mean!"

"Do you know where his mama lives?" Kodak asked.

"Don't rightly know. One payday she don't come around.

Johnny says she just disappeared. Run off with some salesman. Don't think he ever saw her again. Least not I know of."

Bobby and Kodak waited until Hammer Johnson had finished his I pie and coffee before they thanked him and took him home. They hadn't found out much except that John Beltzer enjoyed killing which meant he would not stop.

"A nickel for your thoughts." Nicole said as she came up behind him. She wrapped her arms around him kissing him on the cheek as she did. Her long brown hair was tied back with a ponytail ribbon. The white Greek captain's hat on her head was cocked slightly to one side. She wore a nautically striped V-neck blue and white sailor's shirt with white duck pants and white deck shoes. A lump formed in Bobby's throat. She got lovelier every time he saw her.

"I was just thinking," he said looking up at her, "of what I was going to do to the lady captain of the boat once I got her out in the middle of Lake Michigan."

"And just what were you going to do to her?" she responded, feigning fear.

"I'm going to ravage her body and then make her walk the plank!" Bobby tried to look serious.

"I can hardly wait!" she said laughing. "Now help me get the gear and we'll shove off. I don't want to keep a good man waiting."

"Aye, Aye captain." Bobby said standing at attention. They walked hand in hand over to where Nicole had parked her cream colored Jaguar. They unloaded enough food booze and gear to support two people lost at sea for at least a week.

"Here you carry my Sea Sack." she said. Her arms were already overflowing.

"What the hell's a Sea Sack?"

"It's kind of like a Captain's briefcase. I keep it snapped in the cockpit close to the wheel. Whatever we need or whatever the Coast Guard requires is in that bag. You want to get home safely don't you?"

"I'll let you know later." he said as he leaned down and kissed her on the lips. "I might never want to come back!"

They walked down the pier to the assigned slip where Big Mac a forty foot Hatteras was moored.

"Big Mac?" Bobby said.

"Your grandfather bought it the year the Big Mac was introduced at McDonalds."

"Makes sense." Bobby said as they boarded. "Guess it sounds better than, The Whopper." Nicole laughed and shook her head at him.

"Cast off." she said.

He untied the lines attached to the hull. In a matter of minutes they were headed out of the harbor. He sat in the pilot house next to Nicole and watched her skillfully maneuver the large craft through the oncoming boat traffic. Once they reached the open water and were well off-shore she shut off the engines.

"Now what did you say you were going to do to the Captain?"

CHAPTER 12

J an Dwyer pulled her yellow Mercedes into the third level parking garage of the Hancock Building off Michigan Ave. She searched for a vacant spot found one and pulled in to wait.

She didn't wait long. The passenger door opened and her informer slid in.

"Jesus!" she said. "Who do you think you are? Deep throat?"

"Cut the cracks! Do you want it or not?" He held a manila envelope in his hand. He waved it in her face as he talked.

"How much?" She was agitated.

"Five hundred dollars."

"You're getting a little stiff you know."

He opened his door.

"OK. OK!" She reached into her purse and pulled out five crisp new one hundred dollar bills and handed them to him. He gave her the envelope and as he got out of the car, she was tearing it open.

"Here's a little tidbit for you for free." She stopped. She was all ears.

"Maggie Hardy received an anonymous cashier's check in the amount of fifty thousand dollars. It was drawn on a bank in Lake Forest. Figure it out. Oh by the way," he said smiling. "it was nice doing business with you."

The typewritten note in the envelope was brief. She leaned back in her seat absorbing what she had just read.

"2222 Sheridan Road." She said as she turned on the ignition and back out of the parking space. "I'll stop at Highwood and have a nice dinner at Froggy's. It's on the way."

CHAPTER 19

The sky was as black as velvet and the stars glittered like diamonds sprinkled against dark cloth. The bright lights of the Chicago skyline twinkled in the distance and made the city look as if it were a magical kingdom rising from the depths of the sea. The skyscrapers emerged like towering citadels reaching to the heavens above.

Bobby stretched out on one of the deck chairs positioned on the boat's aft deck. He sipped the rob roy Nicole had brought him from the bar in the main salon. She joined him for cocktails and had then disappeared into the galley below to prepare their dinner. She had given strict, tongue in cheek orders that she was preparing a surprise and was not to be disturbed. He could hear the rattle of pots and pans as she engrossed herself in the production of some culinary delight.

The dining table she set was elegant to say the least. A gold linen cloth covered the game table sitting in the boat's stern. She had somehow smuggled in baby red roses which were now being used as the centerpiece. The galley had been well stocked with crystal silver and special dinnerware trimmed in deep red and embossed with McDonald's unmistakable golden arches and the name of the boat. Long white, tapered candles flickered in the cool, night air.

She had also smuggled in some other necessities such as the soft white terrycloth robe he was wearing. The pocket was monogrammed with large navy blue letters RAC. The matching navy blue swim shorts displayed the same monogram only done in white. She had even thought of topsiders to fit his large size twelve feet.

He took a deep breath, filling his lungs with the fresh sea air. He loved the smell of the water and the slight rocking movement beneath him that came from the sea. It reminded him of voyages he'd made as a young boy with his dad on the 600 foot iron ore freighter his father had commanded. At night when everyone was asleep except the night watch, he used to sneak up topside and lay on the deck and stare at the endless stars that danced in the sky.

He couldn't remember ever being happier than he was this moment, here with her. They had already made love twice today. Each time filled with unrelenting shameless passion and desire. Afterwards they lay embraced in each other's arms totally spent, fulfilled.

Shirley Bassey's lusty voice singing 'And I Love You So' sprang from the ship's built-in stereo speakers to saturate the eerie stillness at open sea. He could hear Nicole, who was still in the galley, singing along with the lyrics. He fingered the silver chain and pendant he had hidden in his pocket. She wasn't the only one who could smuggle something aboard.

"Close your eyes." he heard her say coming up from the galley.

"Close my eyes?"

"Yes. Close your eyes and don't open them until I say. OK?"

He couldn't contain the grin that spread across his face.

"OK, if it will make you happy." He shut his eyes. He could hear her moving up and down the stairs. He could smell the food she was bringing out. Whatever it was it smelled wonderful.

"OK. Open your eyes."

He stared at the feast that set before him. Beef Wellington surrounded with parsley-buttered potatoes and glazed baby carrots filled a large silver tray. Salad plates were heaped with a freshly made Caesar salad topped with anchovies. Hot crusty French bread accompanied the salad.

"Fit for a King." he said looking into her sparkling brown eyes. Her face beamed with pleasure. She was dressed in a floor length blue terrycloth caftan. A large red anchor was centered on the front of her robe. Her soft brown hair hung loosely around her shoulders. She wore almost no make-up. Her skin glowed from color a day in the sun had given her. He held out his hand to her. "Prepared by a queen." She took his hand and he pulled her down on his lap. "You know you're going to spoil me if you keep this up."

"You don't know what spoiled is!" she said kissing him teasingly. "Are you ready to dine Monsieur?"

"I'm starving!" He gently pushed her off his lap and patted her on the bottom as she rose. He walked around and pulled the chair out for her. "Madam?" he said.

She sat smiling up at him as he seated her. He bent down and kissed her on the cheek. She poured each a glass of Cabernet Sauvignon. She raised her glass as she stared into his dark blue eyes.

"To us." she said. They clinked their glasses.

"To us." Bobby repeated.

They ate and drank heartily since their appetites had been sharpened by the sea air. When they finished their meal he pushed his chair back from the table.

"I couldn't eat another bite! My compliments to the chef or should I say cheftess?"

"I have pleased my Lord?" she said clasping her hands together and bowing her head like some shy unpretentious eighteenth century English maiden.

"So pleased, in fact," Bobby said as he reached into his pocket and pulled out the long silver chain and pendant, "a nickel for my Nickel." He held the pendant before her.

The expression on her face revealed her delight and surprise. "Oh Bobby!" She held the pendant in the candle light to admire it. It's a . . ."

"It's a buffalo nickel. My father used to collect them. This one was probably his favorite. It's a 1937 three legged buffalo. If you look real close *you* can see the buffalo has only three legs."

"It's lovely!" she said turning it over. The nickel had been encased in silver. Only the buffalo side of the nickel was visible. On the back, engraved in script, were the words, 'Love you, Bobby'. She read it and then looked up at him. Tears glistened in her eyes.

She slipped the necklace over her head and walked over to him and knelt on the floor in front of him. She reached up and held his strong square chin sensuously between her hands. Their eyes locked. Her face showed the emotion she felt. "I love you Bobby."

"I know." His voice was barely a whisper. He lifted her from the floor until their eyes and lips were only inches apart. He wanted to say, "I love you too" when he kissed her but the words got stuck in his throat. His body felt hot. He could hear his heart pounding in his ears. He had never in his entire life uttered those words to another human being, not even to his mother.

Nicole stood reached behind her and unzipped her caftan.

It fell gracefully from her statuesque body to the deck floor. The silver pendant hung between her firm abundant breasts and glimmered in the candlelight.

"Dessert?" she asked with the same impish grin he had grown to know and love.

"You sure know how to top off a meal!"

It was after midnight before they reached the estate. They did not notice the yellow 450SL that was parked inconspicuously across the street when they pulled into the long private driveway. Nor did they see the burning ash of the cigarette that was held by the individual hiding in the shadows on the patio grounds watching them. They didn't see her. But she was there.

CHAPTER 20

Carolyn Morton was getting used to the teary good-byes she to endured every time she left her mother's home in Libertyville. Libertyville was a small town in the northern suburbs of Chicago where she grew up. Her mother and father had been divorced for six years by the time she reached her early teens. Her mother was in her late forties and still very attractive but had taken the divorce hard. She clung to Carolyn with all the possessiveness of a mother grizzly protecting its cub. When she finished college her mother pleaded with her to move back home, rent free. She would do anything to try to keep her daughter close.

But Carolyn wanted to be on her own and refused her mother's offer. She felt that maybe if her mother did not have her to lean on or depend on she might get back into the mainstream of life. Before Carolyn was born she worked as a copy writer for an ad agency in downtown Chicago. According to Carolyn's father she'd been very good at that job. But now she refused to leave the sanctuary of the house and seemed to be living vicariously through her daughter's life. She avoided all contact with the real world. It took a lot of determination on Carolyn's behalf to sever those ties and to move into her own apartment. She and her old school chum, Debbie Carson, had pooled all their money and found a charming two bedroom apartment in the town of Wheeling about twenty-five miles from Carolyn's mother. Carolyn's father, who still felt guilty about abandoning Carolyn, always contributed money whenever Carolyn asked. However her mother always tried to make her feel that she'd moved to the other side of the world.

Her mother had refused to come visit her which was probably just as well. When she and Debbie rented the apartment four months ago it was just an empty shell. Finances had been tight even with her father's help. For the first two weeks, for lack of beds, they slept in sleeping bags on the floor. Every weekend she and Debbie would hit the garage sales listed in the paper and little by little the apartment began to take shape. They were both very proud of their shoestring decorating efforts.

Sundays were normally reserved for garage sales.

However Debbie had left for Boulder Colorado to spend her annual vacation with her mom and dad who had moved there two years ago. Since Debbie was out of town Carolyn decided it would be a good time to visit her mother. She usually tried to take Debbie with her on these visits since her mother seemed to hold up better in the presence of a third party. It was only when Carolyn went alone, like today, that her mother would try to pressure her into returning home to live. She always tried to make Carolyn feel guilty about wanting to live on her own.

Since she had grown up in the northern suburbs Carolyn always enjoyed the serene scenery of the sprawling wooded countryside that separated each small town. She preferred traveling the back roads rather than the crowded superhighways. She hadn't gone far when she spotted a Garage Sale sign posted on the road next to a gravel driveway. It led to a white farm house which sat back far off the road.

She automatically stopped the car and slowly proceeded down the narrow tree-lined lane. Small stones bounced off the wheels as she drove. She saw a second sign on the driveway that said IN THE BARN. She did not see the bright black eyes that followed her progress down the driveway. Nor did she see the GARAGE SALE sign fall flat in the dirt when a well concealed rope pulled it down. With the sign down all indication of a garage sale was eradicated and so was Carolyn's existence.

It would be almost two weeks before she was reported missing.

CHAPTER 21

obby had become a familiar face around 'Le Fleur' and was now greeted heartily by the entire staff. He would often meet Nicole there after leaving headquarters so the two of them could enjoy a late dinner together after the dinner rush was over. Tonight he had arrived earlier than usual. There was a line of people waiting at the hostess podium to be seated. Nicole was busy taking names and sending them to the bar to wait until their names were called. Bobby walked past her giving her a wink and a smile as he joined the people waiting at the bar upstairs. Big John spotted him as he appeared at the top of the stairs and had a Grant's on the rocks waiting for him by the time he sat down.

"Hi Bobby. How are you doing tonight?" Big John said as he sat down at the bar.

"Not bad Big John. Not bad. Looks like you've got a full house tonight." Bobby looked around the room. Two cocktail waitresses dressed as French maids rustled as they moved around the lounge taking drink orders.

"Just another wild weekend." Big John replied laughing. "People aren't happy unless they're herded together like sheep. Excuse me." He said noticing that one of the cocktail waitresses was waiting to have her drink order filled.

For the next couple of hours Bobby sat watching the people come and go. Occasionally Nicole would steal a few free moments and join him for some brief conversation before she returned to the hectic activity in the dining rooms downstairs.

The bar had just about cleared when a middle aged man sat down next to Bobby. He had a full head of silver white hair and the trim athletic body of a man half his age. Big John greeted him as he would an old friend.

"Dan." Big John said extending his hand. "Where have you been keeping yourself? You haven't been in for a while."

"Just been busier than hell John. Haven't even had time to scratch a good itch. Decided tonight I needed some R and R."

"That a boy. Want your usual?"

"Please. And besides scuttlebutt has it my girl's got herself a fellow. Wanted to check him out. Nobody's good enough for my girl!" He half heartedly pounded his fist on the bar.

Big John chuckled as he poured a Jack Daniel's on the rocks and set it down in front of him. "Well there's no time like the present. Dan McKay I'd like you to meet Bobby Cash. Nickel's fellow."

"Christ!" Dan said flustered. He turned to Bobby who was sitting next to him. "You'd think an old fool like me would know when to keep his mouth shut. I'm sorry . . . ."

Bobby stopped him and held out his hand. "Nothing to be sorry about. I'm glad someone's looking after my girl. Nice to meet you."

Can I buy you a drink? Dan asked still trying to recover from his embarrassment.

"No thanks. Big John put Dan's drink on my check. Loyalty like his should not go unrewarded."

"Why thank you." Dan said as he held his glass up in a salute.

"I understand you're a cop." Dan McKay said after he'd taken a drink.

"Your sources are good. I'm with the Chicago Police Department, Inspector of Homicide."

Dan McKay almost spit his drink out. "Don't tell me you're that Bobby Cash. The one that's heading 'The Chicago Butcher' investigation."

"One and the same." Bobby replied.

"Well for Christ sake. Now I do feel foolish. I've been receiving your department's bulletins. I'm the Sheriff of Lake County." They looked at each other and both broke out laughing. "You'd think an old flatfoot like me could have put two and two together. Here's to you Inspector Cash." he said raising his glass. "From what I hear about you Nickel couldn't be in better hands."

She came up behind the two of them just as they were raising their glasses in a toast. She stood between them and put her arms over both their shoulders. "well it looks like my two favorite men have met."

"We certainly have," Dan McKay said, "and all I can tell you young lady is that you have excellent taste in men."

"I'll second that." Bobby said as he kissed Nicole on the cheek.

"What I want to know young lady," Dan McKay continued as he put both of his hands around Nicole's waist, "is how you managed to snag CPD's boy wonder?"

"Boy wonder?" She said smiling at Bobby.

"Hell I remember the big to do in all the papers, 'Young Boy Wonder Heads Homicide.' He was the youngest officer ever promoted to head a department in the history of the CPD."

"Well I'll tell you all about it under one condition."

Nicole said beaming with pride.

"What's that?"

"That you join us for dinner."

"If I'm not imposing it would be a pleasure."

"I'll set an extra place." she replied lovingly pinching his chin. "It will just be a few minutes."

Bobby and Dan watched her leave.

"One hell of a woman!" Dan said.

"My thoughts exactly." Bobby replied.

They sat in, as Bobby called it, the plaid room. Most of the diners had left for the evening so they had the place pretty much to themselves. Nicole had ordered the special of the evening, Duck L'Orange for all of them. The waiter served a 78 Poilly Fuisse to complement their meal.

When the waiter left and they had settled down to enjoy their meal Dan McKay said, "OK, now I want to hear all about how the two of you met."

Nicole and Bobby over the course of the meal explained about Bobby's grandparents, his grandmother's death, and everything that had brought the two of them together.

"It's just damn fate!" Dan McKay said. "Everything that happens in life is fate."

"I don't know if it's fate or not." Bobby said reaching for Nicole's hand. "All I know is that I've never been happier in my life."

"Nor I." She added. She leaned over and kissed Bobby gently on the lips. When their eyes met, even Dan McKay could feel the electricity that flowed between the two of them.

"Now if you gentlemen will excuse me I've got to help my customers check out. I'll be back shortly." She stood up. "Can I get either of you dessert or coffee?"

Both Dan and Bobby passed on dessert but opted for coffee and a Remy Martin. When the brandy arrived, Dan McKay turned to Bobby.

"If I can ask, what's the latest development on 'The Butcher' case?"

"Not much I can tell you Dan except this guy is smart. And he likes to kill. Which is obvious."

"It was a shame about that detective that got it. What was his name? Hardy?"

"Yes. Mike Hardy. Nice guy. The papers didn't get half the story either. The son-of-a-bitch cut off his head and stuffed it in a wastepaper basket."

"The hell you say!"

"And the worst thing of all is we don't have a single clue as to where he is. Nothing!" Bobby said in disgust. "Mike Hardy was a good cop. One of the best! No one deserves to die like that. No one!"

"Well at least you know who the guy is. Right?"

"We've got a name, John Beltzer. He worked in the stock yards for years. Came from a real fucked up home. His mother was nothing more than a whore. From what we have been able to find out she tried to screw all his co-workers. Could have even been screwing him for all we know. Last thing we know is that she ran off with Beltzer's boss." Bobby frowned. "Now let's get off shop talk. Since you know all about Nicole and me, I want to know all about you and Nicole. I'm sort of a jealous guy."

Dan McKay was flattered. "Nickel and I go back a long way. I'm surprised she hasn't told you about me and her dad."

"She told me a lot about her dad. I'm sorry I never got to meet the man. I think I would have liked him."

"Undoubtedly. He was special. Thought the world of Nickel. I don't think there was anything he wouldn't have done for her. I met him when he was in the contracting business. He was doing a job for your grandmother. Remodeling the coach house that Nickel now lives in. Your grandfather had suffered a stroke and your grandmother decided that she needed someone to help her care for your grandfather. She didn't want anybody living in the house with them so she thought if she fixed up the coach house she could hire a couple to help her out. I knew your grandparents quite a long time too, ever since they moved to the county. I was the deputy then. I used to stop by every once and a while to see how they were doing. That's when I met Nickel's father. I used to love to watch him work. He took that nothing coach house and turned it into a House Beautiful advertisement. I'd try to stop by every chance I could to watch the progress. Each time the transformation was amazing. It was like watching a butterfly emerge from its cocoon. Nickel's Father could work with wood just like a sculptor chiseling granite. We got to be pretty good friends and every once and a while Nicole would bring him lunch, and oh the lunches she would fix. I've never in my life seen anything like them. After a while she started bringing enough for the two of us. Some days I thought I'd died and gone to heaven. I really looked forward to those lunches. Anyway we became good friends and when Nickel's Father died I just felt the need to watch over her like I think her father would have wanted me to. It's become a habit with me now. If I had been fifteen years younger, and single, I'd have probably tried to snatch her up for myself. But I'm sorry to say she's never thought of me as more than an uncle."

"Lucky for me." Bobby replied.

Dan smiled. "It's really good to see Nickel so happy. In all the years I've known her she's had little time for anything but work. Never found that special someone—that is, until now."

Now it was Bobby's turn to be embarrassed. "She's the one who's special." That's all Bobby could say. He was at a loss for words. Nicole joined them just in time to break the awkward silence between them.

"Did Dan tell you all about his relationship with my father and me? He's always been like an uncle to me."

Bobby and Dan both broke into big grins. "See what I told you?" Dan said as he threw his hands up in the air in a gesture of defeat.

"What's so funny?" Nicole said. "I feel like I missed something."

"You didn't miss anything." Dan said still grinning.

"No nothing." Bobby added. "We just missed you."

She knew there was some secret between them since they were both acting like mischievous school boys but she was pleased they seemed to be getting along so well. "Well coming from the two most important men in my life that's quite a compliment. I'm one lucky girl."

"We're the lucky ones." Bobby and Dan responded simultaneously. They all broke into laughter. By the end of the evening Bobby and Dan McKay had become good friends.

CHAPTER 22

The 1978 light-blue Honda slid down the steep embankment and into the flooded gravel pit. John Beltzer watched the bubbles emerge as the small car sank into the dark still water. He smiled to himself pleased as the watery grave closed around the car and Carolyn Morton's mutilated body, concealing all signs of her existence.

The pit was located on a section of land at the rear of the farm's two hundred and twenty acres far from the prying eyes of any intruders. John Beltzer had been here many times before with old man Bates. He had used his brother's barn as a warehouse for some of the junk he had collected for Trash and Treasures.

John now stood at the pit's edge and glared at the water until the bubbles stopped and the surface became motionless. Then he turned and walked down the narrow dirt road. The early morning sun reflected brightly off his freshly shaven head.

The green pastures were dotted with golden mustard flowers and bright purple cock-a-burrs which were pretty to the eye but painful to the touch. When John was about half way down the dirt road, he stopped and turned to look back at the giant oak trees that swallowed the narrow road as well as the gravel pit at the end of it. He squealed with delight and began to dance a little jig in the middle of the dusty dirt road. His secret was safe.

He was lucky to have met old man Bates he thought to himself as he continued his walk back to the farm house. He had met him shortly after the stockyards closed, just after he had lost his job. He was sitting on the stoop of the four story apartment building where he lived when a beat-up old truck, loaded to the hilt with furniture and junk, started to sputter and cough before it finally stopped on the other side of the street in front of him. Steam was pouring from its hood. The driver, a thin tiny old man, got out of the truck and popped the hood. While he was determining the condition of the aged engine John went to fill a bucket with water to bring to the truck. Before old man Bates had assessed the problem John arrived with the water. In the time it took the engine to cool down sufficiently so that the water could safely be added to the overheated radiator old man Bates had offered John a job at Trash and Treasures. He told John that his arthritis was getting worse so he needed someone to help out. John thought the old man was decent enough and he was excited about bringing in a weekly paycheck once gain.

He quickly learned, however, that working for old man Bates was not easy, and that the old man's temperament was far from easygoing. Bates seemed to take particular delight in trying to embarrass John in front of the customers. He would call him stupid and tell him he was a lazy good for nothing slob.

And Bates was stingy. He paid only minimum wage and sometimes not even that. When John had asked Bates for an advance of $65 because he was going to be evicted from his apartment if he didn't come up with the back rent, old man Bates laughed and said that it was fools like him, who didn't know how to save a dime, who would probably end up in the street. He wouldn't give John the $65. Instead he told him he could sleep on a cot in the back room and that he would only deduct $15 a month from John's paycheck.

John hated every day he worked with the old man but he learned the junk business which at times could be very profitable. Since he knew where old man Bates stashed some of his cash he would help himself to a few extra dollars from time to time. As the years passed his resentment for the old man grew until it possessed him like a demon. At night as he lay in the shaky old army cot and plan the old man's detailed and painful execution over and over again in his mind.

When old man Bates' brother died John knew that the old man didn't have a relative left in the world he decided to turn his fantasy into reality. He put his plan into action over a Labor Day weekend. Most shops in the area were closed for the long weekend. Old man Bates had told John that he was going to spend the weekend on his newly inherited farm.

He was packing a few things in his suitcase when John silently came up behind him and raised a solid oak meat tenderizer high above the old man's head. He brought it down hard hoping it wouldn't be a killing blow since he didn't want the old man dead yet. Not yet!

Old man Bates fell hard over the top of the unpacked suitcase. John leaned over him and listened for sounds of breathing. He was pleased when he discovered that the old man was still alive. In the next hour John stripped the old man of his clothes and tied his unconscious body upright in one of the odd chairs that were stacked in the building.

While he sat across from the old man waiting for him to regain consciousness he grinned. He looked over the old man's skinny, bony old body. His body looked even skinnier without the protective layer of clothing. When old man

Bates finally regained consciousness his eyes opened wide with horror. The gag in his mouth prevented his pleas for mercy from being heard. Only the sound of his whimpering could be heard over the next two days as John tortured him. He gave the old man a lot of credit for being as tough as he was for he refused to sign over the business and the farm even when John cut off the top of his left ear with a butcher knife. But he finally succumbed when John slit one of his balls with a straight razor and threw salt in the raw wound. He'd watched pigs being gelded like that in the stockyards. He remembered how the pigs would take off running, squealing in pain. He used to get such a kick out of watching them run around and around the pens bumping into each other with nowhere to go and no way to ease their suffering. He had to admit that he had learned a lot while working there.

Old man Bates squealed as best he could with that rag stuffed in his mouth. He had nowhere to go either. The dead give away were the tears that ran down his cheeks. John finally knew he had him where he wanted him when he held the old man's remaining testicle in one hand and the straight razor in the other.

"I'll give you one more chance old man. Are you going to sign the papers or ain't ya?"

The old man nodded his head in a yes motion.

John untied him and helped him locate the papers he had hidden in the safe in the back room. Slowly and painfully the old man signed the documents putting everything in John Beltzer's name. When he was done he put his head between his hands leaned down on the desk and cried.

But before the old man could react John quickly wrapped a rope around his body and once again bound him in the chair.

"Please!" the old man begged. "Let me go. I won't tell no one. I promise. Everything's yours. It's all legal. Please!"

John didn't answer him but instead, stuck the rag back in the old man's mouth. He pulled out the razor he had been hiding behind his back. "Don't you know old man that the job's not finished until you cut off both balls." Johnny's face was effervescent as he held the razor in front of the old man's face. The sun's rays reflected off the stainless steel blade and glared brightly into the old man's terrified eyes making him squint.

John wanted to have a little fun with the old man before he killed him. After all, he thought to himself, there was no need to kill him with just one swing of the razor.

CHAPTER 23

S everal homicides were reported over the next few weeks. None were considered to be related to the John Beltzer case. It seemed that John Beltzer had disappeared without a trace. One of the recent homicides involved the garroted body of a wealthy New York businessman, Art Benson. Benson had been staying at the downtown Conrad Hilton with his fourth wife of eight months.

Bobby and Kodak were sure that the wife, who had a previous shoplifting and prostitution arrest record, was involved in the murder. She had been caught in a series of lies that made her look suspicious. Her husband had been found dead on a stairwell in the hotel at about 4:30 P.M. A nylon garrote with wooden knobs was imbedded deep in his throat. It was the type of killing that could not be expected by the average burglar. Benson's brown alligator skin wallet, a diamond pinky ring, and his wedding ring were missing. The wallet, which was identified by his wife, had been found in the hotel parking lot. About three hundred and fifty dollars cash had been taken. According to Mrs. Benson all of his credit cards were still there.

Barbara Ann Benson, a flashy blonde, was at least twenty years younger than the victim. She told the police that she had gone down to the coffee shop earlier that morning for a cup of coffee. She said that she hadn't signed a guest check since she had paid the eighty six cents bill in cash. No one from the coffee shop could remember seeing her. That alone seemed suspicious. Usually someone with her looks would be noticed, even in a crowded room. She also claimed that she had returned to the room, put on her swim suit and robe, kissed her husband good-bye, and went to the hotel pool for a swim. Her husband had said he would join her there later.

According to her, when her husband didn't show up, she returned to their room and found the door locked. When she knocked on the door she got no response so she went down to the hotel lobby to get another key from the desk clerk. She returned, opened the door to their room, and called for her husband. According to her, he did not answer but the desk he had been working at was still covered with his papers. She said she stayed in the room for the rest of the afternoon and then ordered a hot fudge sundae from room service while she waited for her husband to return. She thought it was strange that her husband hadn't left her a note as he usually did.

A room service check showed that two hot fudge sundaes had been delivered to the room possibly indicating that she had not been alone. When questioned about it she said the two sundaes had been delivered by mistake and that she had sent one back. It took another day of investigation to discover that the waiter had eaten the other sundae on the way back from her room but had not turned the credit into the restaurant to have the charge removed from the room service bill.

That part of her story had checked out but other parts didn't. The front desk said they had delivered a message to her at the pool at about 10:30 A.M. The message said that Joanie and Jackie would be arriving at about 12:30 P.M. Her husband had died sometime between noon and 2:00 P.M. Mrs. Benson denied ever getting such a message and stated that she knew no one by those names. Several credit card calls were traced to her ex-husband who was living in Los Angeles. The calls had all been placed that morning. She claimed that her ex-husband had cancer and that she had been concerned about him. He was contacted by the L.A.P.D. and was said to be in excellent health.

Art Benson's son, by a previous marriage, said that his father had told him several days prior that he was going to divorce Barbara and return to his third wife.

Bobby and Kodak were sure that Barbara Benson had either hired a killer or that she and a killer had conspired in the death of her husband. There were four telephone calls made to a public phone booth in New York City. The calls had been placed, person to person, to a Jake Marino. However no one by that name could be traced to that number since it was a pay phone. Barbara had stated that the calls must have been charged to her credit card by mistake. Again, she stated that she knew no such person.

The lady had been very cool. She had surrounded herself with a couple of high priced-lawyers from New York who had threatened the Chicago Police Department with a harassment charge. They stressed that she was either to be charged or be left alone—that she had endured enough. She was not charged. She stood to inherit eight million dollars from her husband's estate and unless she was convicted she would get it.

Bobby and Kodak had almost given up hope of solving the case when of fate intervened. An early morning car crash on a foggy stretch of the upper New York State turnpike claimed the lives of five people. A man by the name of Jake Cappelli, alias Joey Fuchs, died in the crash. A State trooper, going through the man/s wallet, recognized a picture of the victim and Barbara Ann Benson. There was another picture of her alone which she had signed on the back. The trooper instantly recognized her from photos that were appearing in the New York papers. The victim of the car crash was also wearing a diamond pinky ring which had been reported stolen.

Bobby issued a warrant for the arrest of Barbara Ann Benson. She was charged with first degree murder. He and Kodak arranged extradition papers to be sent to the State of New York. They had finally nailed her. They were just returning from the courthouse when they received a message from Walt asking them to meet him at the morgue as soon as possible.

Kodak opted to wait in the car when they arrived at the morgue. He watched Bobby walk into the building. He noticed that over the last month Bobby's appearance and attitude had changed. His clothing alone showed a drastic change. Bobby had gone from an early Robert Hall and Levi Strauss to modern and classy Hickey Freeman and Christian Dior. Kodak also noticed that Bobby, who had never been one for jewelry, was now wearing what appeared to be a heavy gold bracelet and watch. He even smelled better.

Kodak knew there had to be a woman in his life—a special woman. He tried to get information out of Bobby about her, but he would only smile. He remained as silent and as tight as a clam about her, though once he did say that Kodak would meet her very soon. Kodak had been able to find out that she had a boy's name, he though, Nick. He had overheard Bobby talking on the phone to her about going out for a Big Mac or something like that. Kodak thought that Bobby could at least take her to a better place than McDonald's to eat.

And food, that was another thing. He and Bobby used to eat dinner out quite often. Now Bobby always seemed to be in a hurry to leave the precinct, giving Kodak another reason to think that this particular woman was special. Though Bobby had never admitted that he was on his way to see her Kodak knew he was. If he and Bobby did eat out now, it wasn't McDonald's or Burger King anymore. It was places like Cricket's or the Cape Cod Room and Bobby would order things with Bernaise or Madeira sauce. Even his taste in food had changed.

Another sign was that he was even driving his own car to headquarters in the morning letting Kodak keep the department car. Bobby's car was no ordinary car either. He knew a little about classic cars and the one Bobby had acquired had to be worth some few bucks. It was a 1962 dark cherry Buick Skylark convertible with black leather seats, a big V-8 engine, and a four-on-the-floor Corvette transmission. The car accelerated like and airliner on takeoff. Since the first day Bobby pulled the car into the lot he'd been the talk of the department. He claimed that he got such a good deal on it that he couldn't pass it up. But scuttlebutt was that he'd connected with a real rich bitch who was paying for his timeas they say. This was all said behind his back of course. No one had the guts to say it to his face. Kodak knew it was more than that but he had to think the rich part must be true.

He knew that Bobby didn't have that kind of money. Yet he also knew Bobby was not the kind of man to be kept by a woman either. All he could do was wonder.

When Bobby entered the morgue he checked Walt's office first and then each of the bisecting rooms until he finally found Walt in the process of performing an autopsy on a little girl of about four or five years old.

When Walt saw Bobby enter the room he motioned for him to wait indicating that he'd be with him shortly.

"After all these years, it still tears me apart to do little kids." He said when he had finished. "Poor little thing suffocated in an abandoned refrigerator. I can't understand people leaving those death traps lying around when all they have to do is remove the damn handles to prevent a thing like this from happening. A fucking simple thing to do to save a life." He pushed the small lifeless body back into one of the coolers. "Let's go into my office." He said as he removed his bloodied apron and latex gloves. He threw them both into the disposal bins. "I think we better talk in private."

"What's with all the secrecy?" Bobby said as he and Walt sat down in Walt's office.

"Yesterday the badly decomposed body of a young woman was brought in." Walt paused to fill the bowl of his old briarwood pipe with his own special blend of tobacco. "I was pretty backed up so I didn't get to her until this morning."

Bobby didn't interrupt knowing that Walt would get to the point quickly.

"In my estimation the cause of death was a blow to the head with a blunt instrument. A blunt instrument that leaves a grill shaped pattern in the wound!"

Bobby instantly got the connection. "Where was she found Walt?"

"She was found behind a clump of bushes in the Forest Preserve between the Tri-State Expressway and Dundee Road. A construction worker pulled off the road there to take a leak and found her."

"That's almost in Lake County. Maybe our boy headed north."

"Exactly!" Walt replied. "And that's why I didn't want to go into this over the phone with the leak in the department and all."

"I appreciate that Walt. You were absolutely right in not doing so. Walt," Bobby asked, "how long has she been there?"

"I'd say two, three weeks." Walt got up and walked over to one of his file cabinets. He took out a large manila envelope and threw it on the desk in front of Bobby. "The Highway Patrol got the call. They transferred the victim's remains here. Her clothes were still intact and on the body. Those things," Walt pointed to the envelope, "were lying on the ground, close to the body."

Bobby opened the envelope. He took out an empty red vinyl clutch purse, some cosmetics, a purple comb with large teeth, a used bus ticket from Evansville, Indiana to Chicago, and a small pink address book. Bobby thumbed through the address book. "According to this the owner of this book is a girl by the name of Dorothy Parks."

"The Highway Patrol noted that and said they would run a check on her for you."

"Did they leave me a copy of their report?"

Walt had anticipated the question and handed Bobby the document.

Bobby read the report in silence. When he finished he said, "It's imperative that we keep this one under wraps. I don't want John Beltzer getting tipped off again. As far as he knows he's made a clean get-away. I want him to keep on thinking that! And Walt . . ."

Walt didn't let him finish. "I'm way ahead of you Bobby. My report will be under lock and key and it will stay that way until you tell me differently."

"Thanks." Bobby stood up to leave. "At least we know which way the pervert's headed." He said good-bye and walked back out to join Kodak.

"Well?" Kodak said as Bobby got into the car.

"We just got another sample of John Beltzer's handiwork. She was brought in yesterday by the Highway Patrol. She was found in a Forest Preserve almost in Lake County and she's been there for at least a couple of weeks."

"So he went north." Kodak said.

"Looks that way. That's about all we've got to go on."

"Think he's headed for Canada?"

"Your guess is as good as mine." Bobby replied, "Unless he leaves us a trail of bodies to follow or unless we get real lucky. He could be anywhere!" Bobby thought of Dan McKay in Lake County. It might be smart to contact him. After all that was his territory.

"Kodak." Bobby said. "How about joining me for some nice French food this evening. There's someone I'd like you to meet."

"You don't suppose I could turn you on to a little soul food instead?" Kodak replied teasingly. "You know those French cover their food with those rich sauces so you don't know what you're eating. Hell they even eat horse meat I've heard.

Bobby laughed. "Well if you cut into it and it starts to whinny I promise we'll leave."

Kodak thought he knew what this invitation meant. He was finally going to meet the mystery lady. Then in his best black jive imitation he said, "OK. But if my ancestors could see me nowthey'd be turning their black asses over in their graves, turning white with envy."

"Kodak, Bobby said, "I'm going to turn you into a honky yet!"

They were both laughing as they pulled out of the parking lot something they hadn't done much lately with the Beltzer case going the way it was. And they both needed it.

They passed a C.P.D. meat wagon pulling in, followed by Coffee and a precinct black and white car as they were leaving. The parties nodded in acknowledgment and proceeded their separate ways.

CHAPTER 24

Kodak watched with amazement as Bobby casually tipped the young car attendant at Le Fleur ten dollars. Judging from the way they talked to each other Bobby was more than just an ordinary customer here. What was even more amazing was the car attendant didn't take Bobby's car to the parking lot as he did the other cars. Instead he pulled it up a little so that it was out from under the canopy and not blocking the front doors yet distinctly visible to all incoming patrons. It reminded Kodak of the limos nestled beside the side entrance of the prestigious Drake Hotel downtown. They were parked far enough away to be discreet, yet close enough for the opulence to be obvious to all who passed by.

Though it was still rather early for dinner both dining rooms in the restaurant were nearly full and several couples stood ahead of Bobby and Kodak when they entered the restaurant foyer. Kodak felt a bit uncomfortable in the luxurious surroundings. He peered into the impressive dining rooms located on either side of the hallway as he absently adjusted his shirt collar to make sure that it was lying properly over his sports coat. He was sure that his sports coat cost less than the average dinner in this place.

The woman who stood behind the hostess podium was as elegant as the crystal chandeliers that surrounded her. She was greeting the couple nearest her as if they were old friends being united after a long absence and was assuring them that their table would be ready. She let them know however that they could be seated immediately or have a drink in the upstairs lounge while they waited for the rest of their party to join them. They graciously accepted the latter suggestion and went up to the lounge. It was then that she noticed Bobby and Kodak standing at the back of the line.

"Mr. Cash." She said smiling as she looked beyond the other customers who were standing before her, "Your party is up in the lounge and your table is ready whenever you are."

Bobby returned the smile and thanked her. He and Kodak excused themselves as they passed by the people in front of them to make their way to the lounge. Some of the people were clearly annoyed at being overlooked.

"You come here often?" Kodak asked as they walked upstairs. He was dumbfounded about Bobby's obvious pull around the place. "They sure give you the V.I.P. treatment around here."

"Let's just say I've got an in with the owner." He replied. He threw his arm around Kodak's shoulder as they ascended the steps.

"The only way I'd get treated like that is if I had something on the owner." Kodak muttered to himself.

When they reached the top step, Kodak stopped looked around the room and then gave a soft low whistle. "Is this a piece of work or what! Reminds me of the interior of some luxury cruising ship."

"That's what it's supposed to remind you of."

He spotted Dan McKay sitting by one of the windows. "This way." he said to Kodak as he directed him to the empty chairs located directly across from Dan. "Kodak I'd like you to meet Dan McKay. He's a good friend of mine. He's also the Sheriff of Lake County."

Kodak did a double take and looked at Bobby again before he shook Dan McKay's hand. Now he knew why Bobby wanted him to meet Dan. But he was disappointed that his hunch about meeting the woman in Bobby's life was wrong.

"What a pleasant surprise to finally meet you, Kodak.

Bobby has told me quite a lot about you and your special talent. "Dan shook Kodak's hand.

"Bobby's full of surprises," Kodak said, returning the friendly greeting. "It's a pleasure to meet you." He glanced back at Bobby who was enjoying Kodak's startled expression.

"Good to see you, Dan. Thanks for meeting me on such short notice." He said as he sat down.

"You sounded slightly mysterious on the phone and you know what a curious son-of-a-bitch I can be." Dan answered. Then, laughing, he said. "Besides, I love the food here and who'd turn down an invitation for a free dinner?"

Now Kodak's attention was peaked. Bobby paying for all the dinners? Who did he think he was, Donald Trump? Kodak could hardly believe his ears.

A young attractive cocktail waitress interrupted Kodak's train of thought. "Good evening Mr. Cash. Sheriff McKay. What can I get you gentlemen to drink?" They gave her their drink orders and when she left, they continued their conversation.

"Dan, as you know, our department's had no further clues on the Beltzer case for weeks. The man seemed to vanish into thin air. That is, until this morning."

"You mean you got something on him?" Dan voice rose with excitement.

"Not exactly on him Dan. But another body. Another woman. We're sure he killed her."

"Jesus!" Dan exclaimed. "Who ever said no news is good news."

"Well, in a way it is good news Dan. Now we're pretty sure that he's in your neck of the woods. The victim was found at the county border."

"How come my department wasn't notified?"

"Dan I don't want you to officially notify your department."

"Bobby, I'm afraid you've lost me. We are talking about John Beltzer. "The Butcher!" The mass murderer! Why in God's name don't you want me to put an A.P.B. out on this bastard?"

"When I've talked to you about this case I failed to mention one thing. There's a leak in our department somewhere. Someone is feeding information to the press and it was that information that tipped Beltzer off and enabled him to escape the last time. It was also probably what got Mike Hardy killed. I'll be damned if I'm going to take the chance of that happening again".

Dan started to reply but waited until the cocktail waitress had set their drinks down and turned to leave. When she left he said, "Now I understand your cautiousness Bobby. But I'm only one man. Hardly enough . . . ."

Bobby stopped him before he could continue. "Dan that's not what I mean. I want you to call a special meeting with your deputies. I want them to be given the same details that I am about to give you. But most of all I don't want any of them to reveal any of the information to anyone outside of the department. That should prevent any further leaks. If you turn up anything, give it only to Kodak, Captain Coffee Marino, or myself."

"As far as anyone's concerned we're not even working on the Beltzer case?" Dan said.

"Precisely."

"Got you, Bobby. Now fill me in."

For the next hour, Kodak and Bobby went over the entire case from their first day at the Argos Meat Packing Plant to Walt's examination that morning of the dead woman.

"Tomorrow morning, unofficially, I'll send you copies of everything we've got. Walt's got an open line to the other coroners in the area. He's going to tell them what to look for. They'll report only to him. I want you to go back about three weeks on Missing Person Files for women who disappeared without a real motive, not runaways. You know what I mean, happily married women. Someone who's family can't believe they've disappeared. Maybe we'll get lucky."

"Did someone mention getting lucky?" Kodak looked up to find the same beautiful woman they had seen downstairs earlier when they'd entered the restaurant. She was now standing behind Bobby.

"Hi darling." She said as she bent down and kissed Bobby on the cheek. He turned looked into her eyes, winked and kissed her lightly on the lips.

"Nick, I'd like you to meet Daniel Webster, better known as . . . ."

She finished Bobby's sentence for him. "Kodak I've heard so much about you. I feel as though I already know you."

Kodak stood. "I knew you'd have to be beautiful but words can't do you justice. Bobby's a very lucky man."

"Why, thank you, Kodak. I've been wondering when he was going to bring you to our humble establishment."

"This is your restaurant?"

"Bobby's and mine."

"Bobby's and yours!" Kodak started to laugh. "He told me he had an in with the owner."

"I do Kodak." Bobby replied. "Would I lie to you?"

"No. But you sure are good at keeping secrets." They all laughed.

"Would you gentlemen like to be seated for dinner? Or if you can wait a little while longer, I'll be free to join you if you'd like."

"We'll wait." They all said in unison.

"I was hoping you'd say that!"

CHAPTER 25

Nicole sat up in bed in the darkened bedroom. The dial of the alarm clock on the night stand told her that it was not yet 6:00 A.M. She looked over at Bobby's long lean form concealed beneath a mound of covers. He had not slept well. During the night he continually tossed and turned. His swinging arms had awakened her twice. He had been mumbling in his sleep occasionally shouting obscenities at the demons that pursued him in his dreams.

The police commissioner, as well as the mayor and the media, were pressing hard for arrest and conviction in the John Beltzer case. Jane Dwyer was being especially pertinacious in her bi-weekly editorial on the Chicago P.D's and particularly Inspector Cash's "bungling" of 'The Butcher' murder case. She had even gone so far as to put a square on the front page of the newspaper, similar to ones used to count down the days to Christmas, only hers said, "53 Days Without Arrest Or Conviction And Counting." An empty jail cell was prominently displayed in the background.

Bobby told Nicole everything about Jane Dwyer and her relationship with Michael Mason and about Jane's nickname. Hell hath no fury as the saying goes, Jane Dwyer was a prime example of that. The woman would print anything that would indirectly put the blame on Bobby and she was beginning to gain a lot of support in the city.

Nicole slid out of bed as quietly as she could, trying not to wake him. She slipped into the royal blue oriental robe he had brought her from Chinatown, when he was down there on a murder investigation. A bright fire-breathing dragon adorned the back of the robe. The silk material felt cool against her naked skin. She walked into her dressing room and closed the door before she switched on the light. As she stood in front of the lighted mirror above her dressing table she stared at herself in the glass.

Her dark hair clung in tangled wisps around her face. The red highlights gleamed in the glare of the harsh lights. She opened her robe and stared at her nakedness. The necklace with the buffalo nickel Bobby had given her hung between her heavy breasts. She put a hand over each one, gently feeling the tender, swollen nipples. Her hands moved down to her slightly extended abdomen, searching for any sign of life from the newly formed fetus she was sure was growing inside of her.

She had already missed one period, an uncommon condition in her life, for she was as regular as clockwork. She was positive that she was going to miss the next one too, which was due in a few days. She hadn't experienced any morning sickness, as she supposed she might, except for upchucking a glass of morning orange juice about two weeks ago. She knew that she had to go to a doctor for confirmation of her fears but she just couldn't bring herself to make the appointment.

It was Bobby she was thinking of. What would he say? Do? He had been very frank about his mother's illness and the reasons why he had never married and why he didn't want any children. He was not about to take the chance of bringing a child into the world that might grow up to be a schizophrenic adult. Now that possibility existed. Would he insist that she get an abortion? Could she? She didn't know. She was thirty-eight years old. That in itself was a danger. She hadn't planned to get pregnant. She had been convinced that she was incapable of conceiving in the first place because she had suffered a severe infection in her childhood and the doctor had told her father that there was a very good possibility she might never bear children.

But now that was a distinct possibility. She knew in her heart that she was pregnant. No dying rabbit was going to surprise her with the news. But how did she feel about it? She wasn't sure of that either.

She loved Bobby and although he had never said it only written the words on the back of the nickel he had given her she knew that he loved her. She had never been happier in her life. He made her feel whole. Alive. They had never discussed marriage only joked about it. Their lives were filled with happiness now. They were both at an age where they didn't need material proof of their love or commitment for each other. They were committed. It was as simple as that. She held the nickel tightly between her hands and stared back at herself in the mirror. She nodded her head up and down. Yes she would tell him when the time was right. When the time was perfect!

She washed her face, brushed her teeth and hair and went down to the kitchen to make coffee. As she stood at the kitchen sink filling the coffee pot with water the sun's rays came peeking over the trees. She had always loved early mornings but running a restaurant and keeping such late hours every night prevented her from being an early riser very often.

Every year she closed the restaurant down for a month from just before the July 4th weekend until the first week in August just to give the staff a nice summer vacation and to have the restaurant cleaned from top to bottom by a professional cleaning crew. This year, however, she and Bobby decided to do a little bit of remodeling since business had been so good. Because the popularity of the restaurant had grown an additional dining room was needed to accommodate the influx of new customers.

She and Bobby had decided to extend one side of the old house to make a garden type dining room which would be built on two levels. She planned to decorate the new addition with white wicker furniture and plants. The skylights planned for the addition would give the plants plenty of sunshine. She had picked out upholstery material that reminded her of the 1950's. It consisted of large dark pink peonies and pale lavender lilacs. The material for the table clothes and napkins contained a tender, delicate, white lily of the valley floral design. She planned to decorate the white painted walls with antique decorative floral plates and with any other appropriate antiques she could find before they opened the addition. They had hired landscapers to surround the dining room with trees and shrubbery and a simulated babbling brook was installed to give the diners the feeling they were dining outside on a cheerful summer day, even if it was really a cold winter evening. That final effect, if properly done, would be dramatic. She and Bobby had named the room, "The Greenhouse," and with any luck the job would be completed within the month Le Fleur would be closed.

When the coffee was done she poured herself a cup and then walked out on the patio to enjoy the brilliant sunrise. The patio was cold and damp. She could feel the dew beneath her feet as she stood listening to a symphony of bird songs, coming from the cardinals, blue jays, sparrows, and other birds.

She and Bobby had rented the coach house to a nice young couple from Michigan. The man was to care for the grounds while his wife took care of cleaning the main house. They were both doing an excellent job. The flower gardens that edged the estate were in full bloom providing an amazing blaze of crayola colors. It was hard to imagine, while sitting there, that other people lived close by. It was so quiet and secluded.

A sudden movement in the dense shrubbery at the rear of the estate caught her attention. She stayed completely still watching the bushes where she thought she had seen movement. Then she saw it. A deer. A timid doe peeking through the dense underbrush. She stopped looked straight up at the patio and seemed to stare directly at her. Carefully as if testing the firmness of the ground the doe proceeded to make her way up the lawn towards the house. How beautiful she was! Deer were a common sight in the woods that surrounded Lake Forest. They were treated with loving care by all the residents who lived in the area. She watched the doe for what must have been another fifteen minutes before the sound of Bobby's voice caused her to bound away.

"Nick?" Bobby repeated as he walked into the kitchen.

"I'm out here on the patio. I'll be right there."

Bobby poured himself a cup of coffee and was sitting at the kitchen counter when she entered the room. She came up behind him threw her arms around him and gave him a huge hug. "Morning, handsome." She said.

"Morning, princess." he replied returning her hug. "You certainly are an early riser this morning."

"It's such a beautiful morning I just couldn't help it." She didn't want to mention that his uneasy sleep had wakened her so early. "There was a deer in the back yard a few moments ago. She stood there just as big as you please."

"Yum, venison!" Bobby said teasingly.

"You wouldn't dare!" she said already knowing that he never would.

"Don't you mean I wouldn't deer?"

"Very funny. Drink your coffee wise guy. I'll go get the morning paper. There's nothing like the bad news of the Morning Sun's sensationalism to take the humor out of a marvelous day." she said as she walked through the house and out the front door to where the paper boy had thrown their papers in the driveway. Both papers had been wrapped in plastic to keep them dry in case of rain. She liked The Lake Forest Herald, which seldom, if ever, contained a horror story. It was generally full of local activities, charity functions and society gossip. The only frightening things in it were some of the prices charged by the local merchants.

She nonchalantly opened her paper and was reading an article on the front page about an antique charity bazaar sponsored by the Women's League when she entered the kitchen. She removed the plastic wrap from The Morning Sun and handed the paper to Bobby.

He unfolded the paper. The bold headlines startled him from his drowsiness. He yelled. "FUCK!"

His reaction immediately caused Nicole to give him her undivided attention. She put her paper down and stared over Bobby's shoulder at The Morning Sun's headlines.

CASH'S CACHE?
CHICAGO COP OR LAKE FOREST LOVER?

A large black and white picture was centered under the headlines. It showed Bobby and Nicole embracing on the stern of the Big Mac. The story beneath it was written by Jane Dwyer. Who else!

According to the by-laws of the Chicago Police Department, a police officer employed by the city of Chicago is required to reside within the boundaries of the Chicago city limits. Inspector Robert Cash does not live by these rules. It has come to the attention of this reporter that not only does Inspector Cash reside at a prestigious address in the Lake Forest area but he has also been the recipient of an estate worth approximately three million dollars. This estate was left to him by his grandmother, the late Kathleen McElinney, widow of financier Stanley McElinney.

Is it possible that this newly found fortune has diminished Inspector Cash's dedication to the Chicago Police Force and is responsible for the sloppy investigation of the John Beltzer case? Is it also possible that being the half owner of the elegant 'Le Fleur Restaurant', which was also left him by his wealthy grandmother, demands too much of his time and energy to enable him to fulfill his obligations to the

Police Force and the people of this fair city? Is it coincidence that Maggie Hardy, widow of Detective Mike Hardy, the detective brutally killed by 'The Chicago Butcher', John Beltzer, was anonymously sent a check in the amount of $50,000? Could this money be considered guilt money? Blood money? Who has that kind of money to give away?"

Bobby could not read the rest of the article. He crumbled the paper into a ball and threw it against the kitchen wall. "Christ! She's determined to have my head and she's not particular about how she's does it. She's even got you involved in this."

"Honey," Nicole said as she knelt in front of him, "don't worry about me. I can take care of myself. This woman is trying to destroy your reputation and you can't let her get away with that!"

"There's not much I can do. She has only printed the facts. I can't even call her a liar, and she knows it. I can't deny that I sent that check to Maggie Hardy, because I did!"

Nicole saw that Bobby's eyes were full of pain. She wanted to hold him, tell him everything would be all right, but she didn't know if that was true. She was afraid for him. He was a cop, a dedicated cop, but who would believe that now? She was trying to think of the right words to say to him when the phone rang.

"Hi Dan." She said. "Yes we've seen it. Thanks Dan. Hold on a moment. I'll get him." She handed the phone to Bobby.

"Bobby, I'm sorry. The woman is a cunt! And besides, anybody who reads that article who knows you will know that it's pure piss-water!" Dan spit out the last words.

"I hope the commissioner is as loyal as you are Dan. Thanks for your support."

"You've always got that Bobby. But that's not why I called. I think we might have a lead on the whereabouts of John Beltzer and if we can nail that bastard you can make Jane what's her name eat her words!"

Bobby forgot the article, concentrating instead on what Dan had just said. "What have you got?"

"There's this girl by the name of Carolyn Morton whose mother called our office yesterday to report her missing. She has been trying to reach her daughter for the last two weeks. But because they didn't have a real good mother-daughter relationship she felt her daughter was just trying to avoid her. The day before yesterday was the day reserved for her daughters normally scheduled visit. When her daughter didn't show up Mrs. Morton called the apartment where her daughter lives. Her roommate, who had just returned from Denver, answered the phone. She told Carolyn's mother that the mail had not been picked up and that two weeks worth of papers were piled in front of the door. She said that she had assumed that Carolyn had gone to stay with her for awhile, that is, until Carolyn's mother called and wanted to talk to Carolyn. Then they both knew that something was wrong.

"I'm going over to talk to the roommate later this morning. I thought you might want to come along. It could be nothing and it could be completely unrelated to the case but this girl just disappeared and as far as her roommate and her mother are concerned she had no reason to."

"Just tell me where you want me to meet you Dan. I'll be there."

"The roommate lives on Wolf Road in the city of Wheeling. It's out of my district but I've already cleared it with the local Police Department since the victim's mother lives in my district. I told the roommate, Debbie Carson, that I'd be there about 11:00 A.M. She lives at the Marvin Garden Apartments. Apartment 14C."

"I'll meet you there, Dan. I want Kodak to come along. He never misses anything."

"Fine. See you there." He hung up.

Bobby quickly called Kodak and explained the situation to him. Kodak had also read the paper and was very apologetic. Bobby didn't want apologies, he wanted facts. It was the only way he could keep his good name.

CHAPTER 26

I t took Kodak well over an hour to reach the house in Lake Forest. Bobby asked him to pick him up so that he wouldn't have to drive his classic convertible to headquarters later in the day, especially because of the article that had appeared in the mornings paper. He didn't want to add any more fuel to the fire.

While Bobby and Nicole waited for Kodak to arrive the phone literally rang off the hook. One of the calls was a directive from the Police Commissioner for Bobby to be at the Commissioner's office promptly at 2:00 P.M. that afternoon. He didn't have to guess what that meeting was going to be about. The rest of the calls were mainly from the press, though God only knew how they got the number. After all it was the only piece of information about him that Jane Dwyer left out of her article. Finally, out of desperation, Nicole just took the phone off the hook.

Although Kodak had been at the restaurant several times over the last couple of weeks he had never been to the estate although Bobby had told him the entire story about the inheritance and what he had received from his grandmother. It was the same night that Bobby had introduced him to Dan McKay. He told him the story in confidence and that was the way it would have stayed as far as he was concerned if it hadn't been for that ball-busting Dwyer woman. When he finally arrived at the estate he was just as impressed with the house as he had been with the restaurant.

It would take them about forty-five minutes to reach Wheeling. With any luck they would be right on time for their meeting with Dan and the missing girl's roommate.

As luck would have it they arrived about fifteen minutes early. Marvin Gardens was a small apartment complex that consisted of four separate buildings. Each yellow and white frame two story apartment was connected to the next. The complex looked like the type of apartment one would find on a hilly San Francisco street. Trees lined the two main streets coming into the complex. The streets, Boardwalk and Park Place, were also named after property in the Monopoly board game just as the complex was. Below the stop sign at the intersection was a picture of the mustached Monopoly man in his black and white striped convict suit, pointing a finger at incoming traffic and saying, 'Stop, or go directly to jail!' It was a clever touch.

When Dan arrived the three of them approached the apartment of Debbie Carson. Dan knocked on the door. A petite woman in her twenties answered the door. She had stringy blonde hair and a pasty white complexion.

"Ms. Carson?" Dan asked.

"Yes."

"I'm Sheriff Dan McKay of Lake County. I spoke to you and Mrs. Morton on the phone."

"Yes. Please come in."

Once they were inside Dan introduced Bobby and Kodak to the nervous young woman. She sat down on the couch, wringing her hands as they talked.

"I really don't know what to tell you," she began. "I was in Denver, as I told you, visiting my parents. I saw Carolyn the day I left. She teased me about jumping ship so I wouldn't have to go on her 'duty' trip to see her mom the next day. Carolyn's mom is kind of overbearing and Carolyn always dreaded having to go there alone."

"Was Carolyn having any other personal problems that might have made her want to just chuck it all and walk out?"

"Heavens no! We've known each other for a long time. The only problem she was having was with her job. She had asked for a raise and they had refused to give it to her. She felt she deserved one so she was looking for a better job."

"Did she have any boyfriends? Lovers?" Bobby asked.

Debbie Carson nearly blushed. "Absolutely not! She wasn't that kind of girl!"

"I didn't mean to imply that she was. Most girls your age have boyfriends. Isn't that true?"

"Yes, I guess, but not Carolyn. She had some pretty bad hang-ups from her parents' divorce and was very stand offish when it came to men."

"Carolyn's mother said that the last time she saw her daughter was two weeks ago Sunday. You said that sometimes you'd go along on these visits. What would normally take place on one of those days?"

"We'll weld usually stop somewhere for lunch before we'd get there. Our favorite place was the lounge at the Pal-Waukee Airport. They make the best hamburgers and French fries around and from the dining room we could watch the small planes take off and land as we ate. After lunch we'd head up to her mother's place in Libertyville. We'd spent several hours talking but mostly listening to Mrs. Morton and when Carolyn couldn't take it any longer, we'd leave."

"How about afterwards? Anything special you'd do?" Any special place you would stop?"

"Nothing in particular. Usually Carolyn would be too upset. Her mother always seemed to have that effect on her. I'd always try to cheer her up on the way home if I could."

"So you always came straight home?"

"Well, not always. Sometimes weld stop for a drink somewhere or hit an occasional garage sale or rummage sale if we happened to pass one. That always seemed to cheer her up. We decorated this whole apartment like that!" she said with much pride.

"Ms. Carson, we'd like to look over Carolyn's personal possessions if it's all right with you."

"Sure. Her bedroom is over here." She got up to show them the way.

The bedroom was sparsely but attractively decorated with a Southwestern theme. Clay pottery, some filled with large paper flowers, Mexican blankets on the walls, and a colorful bedspread decorated the room. Bobby, Dan, and Kodak searched the drawers of her dresser and chest. All her clothes were hung neatly in the closet. The white closet dividers and hangers had helped to keep everything neat. Three pieces of luggage were stacked on one of the shelves. A small jewelry box contained a few gold necklaces and a Seiko watch things the average runaway would take with them.

Kodak went through the trash basket and found a newspaper that was dated from two weeks earlier. Some want ads had been circled. "Maybe one of these potential employers could have talked to her just before she disappeared." he said.

"Take it, Kodak. It's worth checking out. Everything here looks like it's in place. Everybody seen enough?"

They both agreed they had seen enough. They left the bedroom and walked back out to the living room where Debbie Carson was once again sitting on the couch. She seemed to be in a daze.

"Ms. Carson we want to thank you for your cooperation."

She stood and numbly shook her head in acknowledgment.

"If you can think of anything else that might help us find Carolyn, please call us." Dan handed her his card. They started towards the door.

"Oh, and by the way, Ms. Carson," Bobby questioned, turning to face her, "what was the specific reason for the friction between Carolyn and her mother?"

"It was always the same thing." she replied, "Her mother wanted her to move back home because . . . ." Then she stopped before continuing very slowly. "Because she was afraid that something would happen to Carolyn living on her own." She put her hands over mouth. Her wide eyes began to tear as she stared at the three policemen. She realized the significance of what she had said. She began to cry.

CHAPTER 27

S he had called him names, just like his mother used to. Every week, in her column, she would call him more names. And that poor slob, bastard cop, Cash, the one who had tried to catch him. She had even got him suspended. It had all been televised on the six o'clock news yesterday. He watched Cash walk down the steps of city hall, his tail hanging between his legs. Poor bastard.

He would stop her, he thought, as he drove hurriedly along the Chicago streets. He would stop her like he stopped his mother, and he would stop her like he stopped her mother's lover. He would make sure that Jane Dwyer got hers. Just as they got their's!

He passed under a sign that said, '94 South Chicago, Left Lane Only.' He dropped the late model Dodge van into third gear and proceeded slowly down the ramp and onto the expressway. He liked driving the van. It was quite a pleasant change from his old pick-up truck. It had belonged to old man Bates' brother. He considered it just another gift from the old man. He laughed to himself. Yes, he sure was lucky the day he had met the old geezer. That had surely been his lucky day.

But today would not be lucky for some people. Not lucky at all. His thoughts returned to Jane Dwyer. She had to be taught a lesson, just as he had taught his mother and her lover a lesson. A final lesson. He would never forget it. That day burned in his brain like a branding iron on the rump of a Brahman bull.

He remembered he'd been working late in the slaughter house that hot summer evening. Almost everyone there had gone home for the day. His boss and also his mother's lover, Archie Welsh, told him to hose down the floor before he left. Every day he did it, and every day Archie told him again. He thought how stupid he was, repeating himself, like he was talking to a small child. How he hated him. Every time he looked at him, he could see him and his mother's sweaty hot bodies intertwined as they fornicated in her bedroom at their seedy little apartment. Many a time he had come home to hear their grunts of passion. Most of the time neither one had the decency to close the door and John could see their naked bodies bouncing on the squeaky spring mattress. He tried to put the picture of the two of them out of his mind and get back to his work.

Blood from all the slaughtered animals of the day had to be flushed down the drains before it dried and stuck to the concrete making it almost impossible then to remove. He was taking his time as he enjoyed watching the water turn from dark to bright red as it swirled in rushing whirlpools around the many drains in the floor. Besides, he was in no hurry. He had nowhere to go and nothing special to do.

By the time he had finished the job, there wasn't a living soul left in the place. He had just finished winding up the hose and putting it back where it belonged when he heard the voice of Archie behind him. He had come back and he was drunk. It was the same thing he did every payday. Got drunk. Drunk and mean.

"Well, if it isn't Simple Simon." he said, taunting.

"I thought I'd find you here. You're the only dumb son-of-a-bitch that would still be hanging around this stench of death hell hole." His stocky body swayed when he talked and his bulbous nose was as red as his unkempt curly hair on top his head. He held a partially empty gin bottle in his fleshy hand.

"What do you want, Archie?" he asked, turning to face him.

"I just wanted to see what my good-far-nothing asshole peon was up to. Nothing, as usual. Just as I suspected! Low asshole on the totem pole. That's you!" He said, slurring his words, a sadistic grin on his face.

John got up and walked towards him. "Come on Archie. Let's get you home." He took him by the arm, but Archie shook his arm free. "Take your hands off me you bastard" Just like your fucking mother! The no good bitch!" He tried to push John back but lost his balance and fell to the floor before John could catch him. The gin bottle he was holding broke as he hit the floor cutting a deep gash in his hand. He seemed unaware of the cut. Blood slowly seeped from the wound onto the freshly washed concrete.

He looked up at John through stoned glassy eyes. "Well, don't just stand there, you moron. Help me up!"

John looked at him. Archie disgusted him. John hated him, and hated his mother. He wished them both dead. His heart started to pound. The vein in his temple throbbed. Archie was talking to him. John could see his mouth moving but he couldn't hear him. He looked around the room. The knife he used for cutting the throats of the dumb animals was tucked in its sheath on the back wall. He saw himself walking towards it. He grabbed it and held it up high in the air like a Samurai warrior. The sharp stainless steel edge gleamed in the light as he slowly walked back towards Archie, who was still muttering to himself, trying to raise himself, in vain, off the slippery floor.

As Archie struggled to get up, as drunk as he was, he realized what John was thinking as he walked towards him. He watched his eyes that were fixed upon his face, the long knife tightly gripped in his hand. His words choked in his throat. A gurgling, soft, "No! No!" could be heard coming from his lips.

John stood beside him and triumphantly stared down at him the blade of the butcher knife just inches away from Archie's terrified face. He started to say something when suddenly John grabbed him by the hair and jerked his head back. He make one smooth quick movement with the other hand, the same movement he made a hundred times a day. The blade cut easily through three quarters of his neck, severing spinal cord and muscle as it did. Blood gushed in a stream from the severed jugular. He aimed the stream of blood in the direction of the drain and held Archie's head there until it stopped. He didn't want to clean up any more mess than he had too. After all, he'd already washed the floor once today.

He released Archie's limp body and let it fall to the floor. "Now, what to do with you." he thought. He calmly lit a cigarette and walked in circles around the dead body contemplating what he was going to do with it. Then it dawned on him. Today was hot dog day. A day to make plump, fat wieners. The grinder would be full of freshly ground meat! He was in luck.

He hung Archie's body on one of the carcass hooks that hung from the ceiling. He stripped his clothes off and threw them in a pile, but kept his watch and the money he had in his pockets. Not much. But enough to buy a few drinks. He could easy dispose of the clothes later. Then, the same as stripping a steer of its meat, he carefully carved the flesh off the bones. When he finished, he walked the mounds of meat over to the immense meat-grinding machine. He turned it on. Bit by bit, it slowly churned, spitting out Archie's remains with the rest of the ground pork and beef. "I always knew you were a pig, Archie." he said as he watched the last piece enter the huge vat. He couldn't help chuckling. He found it funny that hot dogs were called red hots especially since Archie's nickname was Red. He decided that Archie had come to a just end.

He burned the bones and clothing in the slaughterhouse incinerator. It was designed to turn bones into powder so there would never be any trace of him. Then he got a brilliant idea. Why should Archie and his mother be separated? They truly belonged together. He took the knife washed off the blood and concealed it in his jacket. It was time to go home and finish the job.

He would tell everyone that Archie and the old slut ran off together. Anyone who knew them would believe him. They were always shooting off their mouths about moving to Florida where they could lie on a sandy beach and let their skin cook. "Well, who knows," he laughed out loud. "they might get cooked on some beach after all. We sell our hot dogs everywhere. Even in Florida!" He laughed and laughed again. It was the perfect crime. He was proud of himself. That night, after he got home and murdered his mother, for the first time in a long time he slept like a baby.

He was grinning now as he drove along, just thinking about it. He glanced out the window and realized that he was getting close to the exit ramp that would take him to the Loop. He decided held better focus his attention on the road in front of him rather than dwelling on pleasant memories. He couldn't take the chance of being stopped by a cop for any reason.

He got off on Washington Avenue, knowing that it would take him downtown. The Morning Sun Building was on Michigan Avenue. He didn't know where exactly, but he knew a big building like that wouldn't be hard to find. Before trying to locate it however he would have to find a florist shop or an outdoor flower stand. Either would do.

He got lucky. As he was waiting for the light to turn at the corner of Washington and Dearborn when he spotted a young man walking among the halted cars. The man was trying to sell bunches of roses, six for five dollars. Beltzer picked out a bunch of yellow ones, paid for them, and then drove on.

When he found the Morning Sun Building he circled it until he spotted the employee parking lot. He found an empty parking space about two blocks down and parked. He was wearing a blue jacket with a Chicago Bear's logo embossed on it and a baseball cap. In the back of the van was a jacket he had stolen from Laura's Floral Shop. Its logo was a bunch of spring flowers and the saying, 'Love comes from Laura's florals'. That followed by the phone number. He quickly put on the jacket, left on his baseball cap, and added a pair of dark sunglasses. He popped a stick of gum in his mouth, grabbed the roses, and walked in the direction of the employee parking lot.

A guard stopped him as he tried to walk past the electronically operated wooden barricade that crossed the length of the single-lane entrance. "Hey! You there! Where do you think you're going?" The guard bellowed.

John Beltzer held the roses out in front of him. "I'm supposed to put these on Ms. Dwyer's car. They're a surprise for her."

"Well, you can't go in there. Here, give them to me. I'll do it for you." The guard said as he grabbed the roses.

"Are you sure? Cause I'll get in trouble if they're not put there. This guy gave me good money to make sure she sees them."

"Don't worry about it! I said I'll do it and I will. Now get out of here!"

"OK, OK, I'm going!" John said as he walked back out of the entrance to the parking lot. He ran around the side of the fenced lot and watched the guard walk over to the little yellow Mercedes sports convertible and lay the roses on the dash board. It had worked. Now he knew what kind of car she drove. The rest would be easy.

He returned to the van and circled the area until he found a free parking spot close enough to the building to see the cars coming and going from the Sun's lot. He waited for almost three hours before Jane Dwyer finally left in her car. He crept into the traffic behind her and followed. She didn't go far before she pulled into the circular high rise parking garage of the Hancock Building.

There were several cars between him and her as they slowly made their way up the winding ramps. He saw her pull into a space on the sixth level. He pulled into an empty spot far behind her and waited for the other cars to pass. Instead of getting out of her car she just sat there with the motor running.

It wasn't long before an older, overweight man opened the passenger door and slid into the seat beside her. "Who the hell is he?" John thought to himself. "Could it be her lover?" he wondered. Then out loud he said to himself, "Well, whoever he is, it's his hard luck."

John scanned the sixth level of the parking garage. There wasn't a soul in sight. This wasn't what he had planned, but it would have to do. He gunned the engine of the van. He would only get one chance and he knew it! He released the clutch. The van lunged forward. He could see Jane Dwyer and the mysterious man arguing in the front seat. They were too busy to see him rushing upon them. When they finally did see the van, it was too late.

The front end of John's van slammed into the rear end of the Mercedes. The Mercedes shot forward. The protective retaining wall that lined the parking garage crumbled from the impact. The Mercedes leaped through it and into the open air, six stories high. It fell nose forward, like a missile and exploded on contact with the street below. John Beltzer could feel the heat rising from the flames as he leaned out of the van window and looked down. He felt his penis begin to harden with the excitement of the kill. He would have to take care of that. He unzipped his pants and slowly descended the parking garage exit on the opposite side of the Hancock Building out of sight of the burning vehicle. No one even noticed him. He pulled the van into the first empty alley he could find. Forgetting about what he had just done, he grabbed his hot hard penis with his right hand, closed his eyes, and dreamed.

CHAPTER 28

Bobby sat at the dining room table pushing the rare prime rib around on his plate with his fork. It was normally one of his favorite meals, but not tonight. He was not hungry. He couldn't eat. He could feel Nicole's penetrating eyes fixed on him.

She sat at the other end of the dining room table. Her efforts to cheer him up by preparing a special meal and having a nice romantic evening at home had been wasted. He hadn't been very good company these last few days, not since he had been suspended. He paced around the house and grounds like a caged animal.

Dan Haggerty, the police commissioner, had been very sympathetic yet firm in his decision. Bobby would have to be suspended until internal affairs could further investigate the death of Mike Hardy. Jane Dwyer had intimated that Bobby had not even been aware of Mike Hardy's disappearance for over twenty-four hours. If that could be proven, then charges of negligence would be filed against him. It was a serious offense and could eventually end in his termination as Chief Inspector of the Chicago P.D. Dan Haggerty was also aware of where Bobby lived. He knew that Bobby still maintained an apartment in the city and was required by law to do so. However, since his living arrangements had been made public Dan Haggerty stressed the point that if Bobby was cleared of the charges, which he was sure he would be, he would have to reside within the boundaries of the Chicago City limits. Bobby had mixed emotions over that requirement for it meant that he would not be able to live with Nicole in Lake Forest. He wasn't sure he could comply with that command not even for the Chicago Police Department.

Bobby glanced over at Nicole. The light-blue sequined lounging set she wore sparkled in the candle lit room. With every move she made, it glittered like twinkling stars. He noticed that she too had eaten very little on her plate. She sat holding one leg up on the dining room chair, resting her chin on her knee as she gently whirled a blown crystal glass around in her other hand. The dark red cabernet in the glass swirled in soft waves. For a moment their eyes locked. He wanted to say something but didn't know what. Nicole sensed it and broke the silence.

"Bobby, this is going to work out. I know it is. You said yourself that Commissioner Haggerty knew you'd be cleared of any charges eventually."

"That's the point!" Bobby almost snarled at her and then was sorry for doing so. "I'm sorry. I don't mean to take this out on you. It's just that internal affairs moves with the speed of an old man with a hard-on with buttons on his fly. By the time he gets the buttons undone he forgets why he undid them. And on top of that John Beltzer keeps getting further and further away."

She knew that his feelings of helplessness in the John Beltzer case was the real reason he was so angry. It was becoming a personal thing between him and Beltzer. He had said that Beltzer was making a fool out of him and the entire department and that he couldn't tolerate it. She was about to try to reassure him when the phone rang. She went into the kitchen to answer it.

It was Kodak. Bobby took the call in the den.

"Have you seen the evening news?" Kodak asked.

"No. Should I have?" Bobby responded almost sarcastically. He wondered what they were saying about him now.

"Well, you won't believe what happened. Jane Dwyer is dead. Somebody tried to turn her 450SL into a 727. She took a nose dive off the sixth floor of the Hancock parking garage."

"She was murdered?"

"Looks that way. The skid marks in the garage show that she had help flying through the air."

"When did this happen? Anybody see anything?"

"About two hours ago. No witnesses. The only people there were those attracted by the explosion. She was burnt to a crisp. And she wasn't alone. There was a man with her. Nothing left of him but ashes either. We're sifting through all the debris now hoping we'll find something to help identify the guy. We wouldn't have known it was Dwyer either except that her license plate flew clear of the wreckage and was only partially burned."

"Well, I can't say I'm sorry. With the kind of mouth she had she had her share of enemies, including me. Keep me posted will you? You're the only pipeline I've got left."

"Sure thing Bobby. And Bobby, if there's anything you need, anything at all, don't hesitate to call me. OK?"

Bobby knew that Kodak was sincere. He was about to return to Nicole in the dining room when the phone rang again. This time it was Dan McKay.

"We've got another disappearance only this one's more recent. I'm at their house now. Thought you might like to be in on it."

"Where are you?"

Dan McKay explained where he was. It took Bobby only a half-hour to get there.

CHAPTER 29

J oni, short for Jo Ann, Emerson lived in the woodsy suburb of Hawthorne Woods. The houses there were priced well into the two hundred thousand dollar range, most of them on lots of an acre or more. Joni was considered a housewife, although she sometimes worked at a local antique shop for extra income. She and her husband, Donald, had two grown sons. One Michael, the oldest, still lived at home and was employed by his father, who owned the Emerson Construction Co. The other son, Danny, had just finished his senior year at Ohio State and was in New York for a job interview with Gulf and Western for an electrical engineering position.

Last Sunday had been Donald Emerson's mother's seventy-first birthday. He and Michael had driven fifteen miles southeast to Buffalo Grove where she lived, to take her to the noon Sunday mass at the local Catholic Church. Joni, who never went to church, was going to the Hills Shopping Mall to pick up the microwave oven they bought from Sears Roebuck for Donald's Mother's birthday present and then on the bakery to get the birthday cake they had ordered.

Donald Emerson's brother and sister and their families were to arrive at his mother's house at about 2:00 P.M. to join in the birthday celebration. Joni said that she would be there by the time they all arrived. When she did not arrive by 2:00 P.M. Donald though it curious about her not being there by the time they all arrived. When she did not arrive by 2:30 P.M., Donald though curious about her tardiness, really thought nothing of it. His wife was considered a shopper and sometimes got so carried away in her browsing that she would lose track of time.

But when she still hadn't arrived by 3:00 P.M., Donald became concerned. Joni knew that the family had all agreed on an early dinner and over the years she had always been the coordinator of these functions. It was completely out of character for her to be so late, much less not show up at all.

By 6:00 P.M. the entire family was frantic. Donald's sister called every hospital and every law enforcement agency they could think of in the areas that Donald's wife could possibly have driven through on her way to Buffalo Grove. They all feared the worse that she had been in an automobile accident and had been hurt too badly to have a message relayed to them. When the hospitals came up empty, as a last resort Donald's sister called the morgue. She happily reported to the family that no one matching Joni's description had been brought in all day.

Donald and Michael Emerson returned home to wait for any further news of Joni's disappearance. When she had not returned by early the next morning, Donald called the local police. Though sympathetic, they said that she would have to be missing for twenty-four hours before a missing person's report could be filed.

The Hawthorne Woods Chief of Police had received Dan McKay's memo, which indicated they were to report any unusual female disappearances. Unfortunately he was on a fishing vacation in Wisconsin when the missing report on

Joni Emerson was filed. Josie Emerson's disappearance was indeed unusual. She was missing for five days before Dan McKay was notified.

Though the hour was late, Donald Emerson was completely receptive to meeting with Sheriff McKay and the very tall man he had brought with him. Dan and Bobby had agreed it would be best not to bring Bobby's name into the investigation unless they absolutely had to. They knew that if Donald Emerson recognized Bobby, especially after all the publicity Bobby had received, there would be a good chance Donald might conclude that his wife was in the hands of 'The Butcher.'

When Dan and Bobby entered the two-story traditional Williamsburg house they found an emotionally battered man in his late forties. His son, Michael, sat on the couch in the family room next to his father. His arm was around his father's shoulders, trying to comfort him. It was obvious to Bobby and Dan from the swollen red eyes that both of them had been crying.

They talked with them for a half hour before they went through Joni's personal belongings in the bedroom. They hoped they would find the suitcases gone and that she had run off with another man. They weren't. She hadn't. There was no logical explanation for what could have happened to Joni Emerson. No clues. Dan and Bobby concluded privately that the woman had probably been abducted, that John Beltzer could be responsible.

"Well, what do you think?" Dan asked Bobby as they headed out towards their cars.

"I'm thinking the same thing you are. She's dead."

"Got any ideas?"

"A few." Bobby said. "I'd like to sleep on them. How about if I meet you at your office in the morning. We'll go over them then."

"Fine with me. See you then. Oh and give my love to Nickel."

"Will do." Bobby said. He got into his car and headed for home. It was after 10:00 P.M. before he got there. Nicole was waiting for him when he arrived. She kissed him when he walked in the door.

"How did it go?" she asked.

"A real bitch!" He said returning her kiss. "How about a brandy and I'll tell you all about it."

"You've got a deal! I'll be right back." She walked into the library and poured a healthy portion of DeMontal's Armagnac into a large Waterford snifter.

"Thanks." he said when she handed it to him. He waited for her to get comfortable on the sofa across from him before he began. "I just left a man whose whole life is crumbling before his eyes. He and his wife have been married for twenty-six years. They're both in their late forties. His wife left last Sunday to go to the mall to pick up a microwave oven and a birthday cake for her mother-in-Law's birthday party. It seems she just disappeared off the face of the earth! The local police have tracked her movements on the day she disappeared to Sears Roebuck, where she did pick up the microwave oven. Her husband wasn't sure which bakery she had ordered the cake from so it took a little longer to find the right one. She never picked up the cake. We know that she vanished somewhere between the shopping mall and the bakery, a distance of about ten miles."

"Do you know which route she might have taken? People tend to travel familiar roads."

"My thoughts exactly. Tomorrow morning *I'm* going to meet with Dan and work out a detailed plan of action for covering what should be the possible area of her disappearance, assuming she did leave the shopping center and was on her way to the bakery when she disappeared. If she never left the mall my theory is all wet and Dan's men will just be going on a wild goose chase."

"What about the other girl who disappeared? Was she in that area too?"

"You know, you'd make a damn good detective." He smiled at her proud of her insight. "And to answer your question yes, somewhat, though her route was quite a bit longer distance."

"Then," she said, coming over to sit on his lap, "you're right on track."

"I hope so, Nick. I really hope so."

She put her finger under his chin and raised it so that he was looking directly into her eyes. His blue eyes were sad and full of hurt. "And speaking of being on the right track," she said flirtatiously, "how about you and I making some tracks to the bedroom. I've got a problem that only you can solve."

"I wish all my cases were as easy to solve." He smiled for probably the first time that day. The solemn tightness he felt slowly began to fade. She knew how to take his mind off the gloomy events he had just witnessed. They got up and walked hand in hand up the stairs. When they reached the bedroom they leisurely undressed each other before sinking into the soft champagne-colored down bedspread that covered their bed. Then as if they were making love for the first time each slowly explored the other's body with their tongues and fingers. When they could no longer bear the passionate teasing of flickering tongues and fondling fingers, ardent burning desires squelched their foreplay and only thoughts of total fulfillment consumed them. Their need became suddenly urgent. Demanding.

When they had finished their lovemaking, they lay in each other's arms. Their bodies were wet with perspiration and their chests rose and fell in unison from their labored breathing. They heard the beating of their hearts in their ears.

"Did I say this was easy?" Bobby said, out of breath. "There should be a Surgeon General's warning pasted across your forehead. This passionate woman could be dangerous to your health." He laughed feeling good for the first time in days. "You're going to give me a heart attack yet."

"Oh, but what a way to go!" she responded as she lightly ran her tongue along his cheek and then playfully across the shape of his lips.

The contentment they felt spread through their bodies as completely as the warmth from the brandy they had enjoyed earlier. It wasn't long before Bobby was sound asleep. Nicole watched him for a long time wondering how she was going to gather the courage to tell him she was pregnant. The tests had been positive, as she knew they would be. Before she finally fell asleep she made up her mind that she would tell him in the morning. She couldn't keep it a secret any longer. She was well into her second month already.

CHAPTER 30

She had set the patio table for breakfast. She was seldom up this early but with everything she had on her mind she rose earlier than usual. She did not want Bobby to leave before they had a chance to talk.

He came down shortly before 8:00 A.M. The mood he had been in the day before had lifted and he happily embraced her when he found her in the kitchen preparing pancakes and sausage. Bobby, normally not a breakfast eater, was ravenously hungry this morning probably because he hadn't really eaten any dinner the night before. He lingered around the stove drinking his coffee, playfully fondling her while she prepared their breakfast.

"If you keep this up, we're never going to eat." she said, pretending to be annoyed.

"Who needs food." he said spinning her around pinning her to the stove. "I'm going to ravage your body. Suck your blood!" he exclaimed in a Bela Lugosi like voice sinking his teeth tenderly into the side of her neck like a vampire.

"OK, if you'd rather have that on your pancakes than Aunt Jemima's maple syrup." she giggled as he continued to tickle the side of her neck.

"I'll take Aunt Jemima's, please."

"Then help me bring this out to the patio." She shoved a tray full of pancakes, sausage, butter and syrup into his hands.

"Yes sir." He said saluting her. "Your wish is my command."

"And don't you forget it!" She said mockingly yet lovingly, unable to hold back her smile.

They sat at the patio table eating their breakfast and reading their papers enjoying the still cool morning. It had been in the low eighties yesterday. The humidity was high and the day had been sticky. Today was supposed to be a carbon copy.

"I'm going to drive out to the restaurant this morning to see how they're progressing on the addition. Afterwards, there are some great garage sales I noticed in this morning's paper that I want to hit. I'll need a lot of knickknacks and decorations to cover those blank walls in the new addition. After that I'm going to an antique sale at the Long Grove Tavern. Would you like to meet me there later?"

"I don't have any idea when Dan and I will be finished so I think I'll pass. And besides," he said curling his lips in disgust, "the only people there will be a bunch of rich old ladies trying to spend their husband's hard-earned cash on junk my grandmother would have thrown in the trash."

He was joking and Nicole knew it. But she also knew that he didn't share her love for antiques unless they were nautical. Those he was crazy about.

"OK, have it your way. But you don't know what you're missing." She raised her eyebrows seductively. "Then, how about bringing Dan home for dinner. I'll whip up some mean T-bones on the grill."

"Sounds good to me. I'll ask him."

"Just tell him ice cold martini's will be served promptly at 7:00 P.M. That ought to bring him running."

"If it doesn't bring him it will certainly bring me."

Nicole could tell when Bobby had finished his meal that he was anxious to get going to meet with Dan as he had planned the night before. She knew it was now or never. As he gulped down the remainder of his coffee and was preparing to push his chair away from the table she put her hand over his to stop him.

"Bobby, I have to talk to you about something."

"Can't it wait until this evening? I'd really like to get an early start with Dan this morning. We've got so much to do." He pushed his chair back as if she had already agreed to what he had just asked.

"It will only take a minute. And it's important."

"OK sweetmeat." he said, using one of his pet names for her. "What's on your mind?"

She lowered her eyes unable to meet his gaze. "I don't know how this happened," she said but he impatiently cut her off.

"What is it?" he said not taking his eyes off her.

"I'm pregnant!" She looked up at him searching for his reaction.

His body stiffened. The warm loving blue eyes she had known went cold and seemed to turn to stone. "Nick, you know how I feel about that. I've told you about my mother and why I've never married. You know why I've never wanted children. I still don't. You'll have to have an abortion."

"But Bobby, Doctor McCree assured me that our chances of having a schizophrenic child are minimal."

"That's a chance I'm not willing to take!" He was yelling at her. "Now, you go back to him and tell him you want an abortion."

"I don't know if I can do that! I want our baby. I want to have it!" She was screaming now saying for the first time what she felt deep inside. Tears were streaming down her face. She got up and ran from the patio into the house. Bobby could hear her footsteps as she ran up the stairs to their bedroom. Through the open window he could hear her sobbing.

He was angry with himself for yelling at her and for making her cry. Yet he didn't go to her. If he did she might think that he was giving in. He wouldn't give in. He couldn't. He threw his napkin on the table and pushed his chair back so abruptly that it fell backwards. He didn't pick it up.

His sports coat was upstairs in their bedroom. "The hell with it." he said to himself and started for the front door. The phone rang just as he was walking past the library. He walked in and grabbed it before it could ring a second time.

"What?" He shouted in the receiver.

"Damn." Kodak exclaimed. "You don't have to bite my head off."

"Sorry Kodak. I'm not having a good day."

"Well you will after you hear this." He sounded excited.

"And what's that?" Bobby didn't sound as confident that the news could change his disposition this morning.

"Guess who the guy was who died in the car with Jane Dwyer." Kodak was too excited to wait for a response. "You won't be able to guess. It was Coffee!"

"Coffee? What the hell would Coffee be doing . . . ." Bobby didn't finish his sentence. Then the news made sense to him. Coffee had been the leak. Coffee had been Jane Dwyer's informant! "Well, I'll be a son-of-a-bitch!"

"Can you believe it? Coffee was the leak. The whole department is in shock."

"But why?" Bobby asked still stunned by the news.

"Don't know. Maybe she gave him a lot of money or maybe it was just his way of getting back at you. After all *you* did get the promotion he had expected to get."

"I guess . . . . It's just that I always thought of Coffee as a good cop, even with all the differences we had."

"We'll probably never know the answer. It died with him."

"How did you find out it was Coffee?"

"His badge was found in the rubble and though the numbers were illegible we knew it was from a cop. Then one of the boys got the idea that maybe his car would be parked on the sixth level of the garage somewhere since the two of them were in her car. And bingo! We found Coffee's car."

"It's hard to believe. I never would have guessed it."

"And that's not all." Kodak was even more excited. "I have the pleasure of telling you, unofficially, that you will be reinstated in the department shortly."

"Hot damn!" Bobby shouted. How do you know that?" It seemed as if the weight of the world had just been lifted from his shoulders.

"Because Police Commissioner Haggerty got into the Dwyer case last night. When he realized that the dead man with Dwyer was Coffee he also realized right away that Coffee was the informant. But what we didn't know was that Coffee had secretly testified against you in Mike Hardy's death. His testimony was the only reason the charges were being filed against you. So no Coffee, no charges."

"Well, I'll be damned."

"Commissioner Haggerty said that he will make the announcement officially this afternoon. So my good friend your troubles are over."

Bobby thought of Nick upstairs. "Well, not exactly, but close. By the way, I'm meeting with Dan McKay this morning. I think we're getting somewhere in the Beltzer case."

"Great!" Kodak replied. "Now that would make this a perfect day! Do you mind if I tag along? I'll call in sick."

"You better not let your superior know. You might get the boot."

He laughed heartily. "He'll never know!"

Bobby joined his jolly mood. "OK I'll see *you* at Dan's when you get there. I'm leaving here right now."

"It's a date!" Kodak said and hung up.

Bobby's mood was much better now. He wanted to run upstairs and take Nick in his arms and kiss away her tears. He took a couple of steps in the direction of the stairs then stopped. He couldn't bring himself to do it. Instead, he left through the front door, hopped into his '53 Skylark and drove away. But with every mile he put behind him, between himself and Nick, he had to fight the urge to turn around. To go back to her. To hold her. But he didn't.

For the rest of the day Dan, Kodak, and Bobby went over all the possible routes the two missing women could have traveled. They interviewed clerks at stores along the way, showing them pictures of the missing women, hoping that someone would remember one of them. But they came up empty. Bobby tried to call Nick during the day to sooth things over but there was no answer. He remembered that she was running a lot of errands and because of the way things were when he left her that morning he wasn't sure if he should still ask Dan home for dinner. But he took the chance and decided that her invitation was still good, so he invited him and just to play it safe, he invited Kodak too. She couldn't possibly stay mad at him. Especially in front of guests. At least he hoped not.

CHAPTER 31

Nicole heard the squeal from the tires of Bobby's car as he angrily sped down the driveway. Enraged she grasped the silver pendant that hung around her neck and ripped it off. She flung it against the floor with as much force as she could. Then as she stared at it lying on the floor she broke down into tears.

"Oh Bobby!" she cried. "Why? Why?" she moaned flinging herself across their bed. I love you and I want our baby." she murmured between sobs. Finally she rose from the bed and walked into the bathroom. She stared at her tear-stained face and swollen eyes. She wet a wash-cloth and patted cold water on her hot skin. As the cool water soothed her it also refreshed her spirit and she began to feel less depressed.

She threw the washcloth at her image in the mirror. "I'm sorry Bobby," she said forcefullystaring at herself in the mirror, "but this is my baby as much as yours and I'm going to keep it with or without you!" She swallowed hard thinking about the consequences of her decision. But she had made up her mind and was going to stick to her decision. If it meant Bobby's walking out, then so be it! She could manage with out him. If she had to . . . . She shuddered at the thought of it.

She went downstairs and got a cup of coffee. She still had a restaurant to think of and plenty of work to do. She went over the newspaper want ads as she put on her make-up and got dressed. Going to some garage sales and the Long Grove auction she thought would help to take her mind off Bobby and the baby. She cut out some ads and stuck them in her purse and gave herself one last inspection in the mirror. "Not bad for an old pregnant woman." She said to herself. She had chosen a white linen skirt with a pale peach blouse and a dark peach and shell woven-rope belt to accent her waist. She placed her hands on her hips and twirled back and forththen headed for the door. On her way out she retrieved the broken silver pendant off the floor, gave it a squeeze, and put it in her purse. Somewhere along the way today, she would stop and try to get it fixed.

CHAPTER 32

obby turned into his driveway, Dan followed in a Lake County squad car, and Kodak in one of the city's unmarked cars. If anybody had been watching, they would have thought there was about to be a bust of some kind in the affluent tranquil neighborhood of Forest Lake.

Bobby stopped his car at the front door, and Dan and Kodak stopped their cars behind his. When they got out of their cars, they were grinning as they watched him carry a huge bouquet of yellow roses to the house. In following him to his home they had to wait outside four florist shops until Bobby finally found the yellow roses he was intent on getting. As he was carrying the bouquet to his car he had looked over at the two of them.

"They're what she likes!" Bobby had yelled, defending his search.

Kodak and Dan both laughed and continued to grin all the way to the house.

When Bobby entered the house followed by Dan and Kodak, he was surprised to find it empty. Nicole was not there. After searching for her Bobby went downstairs to find that Dan and Kodak had made themselves comfortable in the library.

"Did she forgive you?" Dan asked, smiling.

"I don't know. She's not here." Bobby replied, puzzled.

"Man, you're in big trouble!" Kodak said. "You're going to need more than roses to straighten this out." He was jesting. "By the way, what did you do?"

Bobby disregarded the question and asked instead. "What can I get you two troublemakers to drink? Hemlock maybe?"

They both smiled at the comment.

"Jack Daniels on the rocks. If you've got it." said Dan.

"Make that two." Kodak added.

Bobby poured the drinks and then sat down on the soft leather couch next to Dan. They began discussing the Chicago Bears and their chances of making it to the Super Bowl the next year. They all agreed that without Jim McMahon the team just wasn't the same.

Bobby noticeably kept glancing at his watch. Dan and Kodak noticed it and knew he was worried.

"Maybe we should go, Bobby." Dan said. "We'll come for dinner another time."

"No!" Bobby said. "Listen, I've got an idea. We'll drive over to Maxwell's and have dinner there. I'll leave a note for Nicole and ask her to join us there when she gets back. She went to some antique auction in Long Grove and you know the way those things can go on and on." Bobby felt upset. There were pangs in his chest. He was hurting inside, something he'd never experienced before. He couldn't wait to see her and damn it if she had her heart set on having this baby then maybe they should!

"Hey, Bobby." Kodak said. "It's no big deal. We'll do it another time."

"The hell we will." Bobby tried to sound convincing. "I'll just write her a note and we'll be on our way."

When Bobby left the library Dan and Kodak were silent. They looked at each other but neither said anything. Bobby wasn't fooling them.

On his way to the kitchen Bobby grabbed the vase that sat on the table in the middle of the foyer. He threw the flowers that were in it into the garbage can, even though they were still quite fresh, and placed the roses he had just bought in the vase instead. He wrote a short note and taped it to the vase. He wanted to make sure she saw it as soon as she walked in the door.

Bobby drove the three of them to Maxwell's, a steak house in downtown Lake Forest. There was always a wait for a table there, even with reservations. They gave their name and were ushered into the bar, where they sat in a booth that faced the door. Every time someone walked through it, Bobby would look up. After about forty-five minutes, they were finally called for dinner.

Dan and Kodak dove into the oversized charbroiled porterhouse steaks. Bobby hardly touched his, claiming a upset stomach. Dan and Kodak both knew that if anything was upset it was Bobby's feelings. Hard as he tried he couldn't cover his disappointment when Nicole failed to join them.

They finally left, skipping dessert, to go straight back to the house. It was pitch black. There wasn't a single light on and Nicole's car was missing from its usual parking spot.

Suddenly Bobby was frightened.

CHAPTER 33

A t times there are obvious advantages to being a cop and having cops for close friends. This was one of those times. After Bobby had checked with Mrs. Lamount, at the coachhouse, Dan got on his car radio and had his department check to see if Nicole had been in an automobile accident. The department quickly checked through the city, county, and state records for the day, matching Nicole's car model and plate number with all reported accidents. She had not been involved in any accident listed on the daily reports. Dan also had the Coast Guard check "Big Mac" to see if Nicole was aboard. She hadn't been seen there either.

Bobby called Le Fleur on the chance that she might have stayed there. When there was no answer, Kodak volunteered to drive over and take a look. Kodak thought Nicole might have gotten sick, passed out, or have even fallen and was unable to get to a phone. Bobby thought of the baby she was carrying inside her. Maybe she did get sick. He was grateful for Kodak's concern. Dan or Kodak knew nothing about the conversation that had taken place that morning. But after thinking about it Bobby called all the hospitals in the area to see if she had been admitted to any of them. Again he struck out.

The Long Grove Tavern was located in the sleepy little town of Long Grove. The town considered itself to be the antique capital of the world. Maybe it was. It was full of little shops overflowing with antiques as well as replicas and old junk. Nicole loved to go to auctions at the tavern. They were famous for their platter-size T-bone steaks but everything on the menu was excellent and dinner was served during the auction. The auctioneer was a jolly man and his antics alone made the evening a treat for all in attendance. Bobby remembered the first time she had talked him into going to one of the weekly auctions. As they were walking in, a middle-aged, well-dressed couple were walking out with their arms full of merchandise. The man said halfheartedly, "Yes sir," he said winking at Bobby, "this dinner only cost me six hundred dollars." They had all laughed. It had been funny at the time. But Bobby found no humor in it now, or in anything else, for that matter.

Dan insisted on driving to the Long Grove Tavern to look for Nicole. He took a picture of her with him to show to the employees. He thought someone might remember seeing her and might know when she had left. Bobby called the auction house to have her paged but the hostess rudely told Bobby their paging system was broken, that they were busy and didn't have the time to search for Nicole or anyone. Bobby told the woman he was with the police. That it was urgent. She said that she had no proof over the phone that he was with the police and hung up.

Dan and Kodak both returned in a couple of hours. Both of them had drawn blanks. For the first time in his career Bobby knew how the family of a missing person felt. He had always been sympathetic, but had never really experienced the agony such a person goes through. Not until now. This time he was the family of a victim.

Nicole didn't have any living family as far as Bobby knew so it wasn't likely that she had sought refuge with a relative because of their argument that morning.

Dan, who loved Nicole like a daughter, felt it was his duty to pin Bobby down about his argument with Nicole. Bobby kept insisting that the argument had nothing to do with the fact she was missing. It wasn't until the wee hours of the morning when Bobby was frantic with worry that he finally told Dan and Kodak everything.

Bobby then told them briefly about his mother and father, about Nicole's pregnancy, and how he had reacted to the news. He regretted it all now and was willing to bargain with the devil, if necessary, just to get her home safely.

Dan and Kodak thought that the best thing to do would be to treat this like any other case and begin at the beginning.

"Bobby, this morning when you and Nickel were having breakfast," Dan couldn't get out of the habit of calling her that, "what exactly did she say she was going to do today? What do you remember?"

"She said that she was going to go to the restaurant to check on the addition we're building and then she was going over to the auction."

"Did she mention anything else?" Dan had to push. He knew that it was the push that sometimes shook the memory a little bit. "Come *on*, Bobby. Think! Think!"

Bobby gave Dan a nasty look. At the moment he resented Dan's badgering him. Bobby wasn't thinking like a cop. He didn't feel like a cop. He felt devastated. He put his head between his hands and shook his head. Then slowly he uncovered his face. "Garage sales! She said she was going to hit some garage sales she had seen in the morning paper!"

"Where's the morning paper? Have you seen it around the house?" Dan was excited now.

Bobby thought. "Upstairs! Upstairs on her dressing table." He ran up the stairs, taking them three at a timer to her dressing room. The newspaper was there. Bobby picked it up. She had cut out four squares from the Garage Sale section. Bobby dashed back downstairs to show Kodak and Dan.

"Here it is!" He showed them the places that were missing. "I'm going to run to town and find a newspaper stand. Then we'll know where she went!" Bobby felt exuberant. He felt hope again.

Kodak put his hand on Bobby's shoulder to stop him from bolting out the door. Dan had a dismal expression on his face. Kodak looked at Dan before he started to talk to Bobby.

"Remember the Morton girl? Her apartment?"

"Yes. So?"

"Remember she was job hunting?"

"Yes," Bobby said abruptly. "will *you* get to the fucking point Kodak? I want to get the fucking newspaper before they take this morning's copy off the street!"

"I took a newspaper from her wastepaper basket.

Remember? The want ads were circled on one side. The side *you* saw." Kodak hesitated. "But garage sales were circled on the other side. At the time I just didn't . . . ."

"Dear Mother of God!" Bobby cried. "John Beltzer!

It's not possible. It couldn't be!" Bobby's heart stuck in his throat. His eyes began to fill with tears. He was visibly shaken. The magnitude of what Kodak had just said, the horror of it, shook Bobby to his soul. "Why didn't we think of that earlier? The man dealt in junk for Christ sake! It makes so much sense. Women disappearing off the face of the earth! I just hope, I pray . . . ." He couldn't say what he was thinking. He didn't even want to think about it.

Dan put his arm around Bobby's shoulders. "We'll find her, Bobby. We don't know for sure that she's been abducted. She could just as easily be holed up in a motel just wanting to teach you a fucking lesson." Dan squeezed Bobby's shoulder and smiled at him. "Which you probably fucking deserve!" Dan wanted to make him feel better, if that was possible. But Bobby just couldn't make himself smile back.

"I've got the newspaper we took from the Morton girl's apartment. It's in the file at the department. I'll go get it," Dan said. "Kodak you run into town and get the Lake Forest paper that Nickel had this morning."

"Who the fuck are you giving orders to?" Bobby's tone startled them. "I said I'd get it and I will!. As for you Kodak you can go with me or get the fuck out of my way!" Bobby's anguish had turned to anger. "I'm going to find her and I'll find her with or without your help!"

"Bobby, Bobby." Dan said. "Calm down. We're not against you for Christ's sake. We'll find her. Just take it easy." It was Dan's turn to raise his voice. "If you want to find her you'd better start thinking like a cop! This is no time to let your emotions get the best of you!"

Bobby knew that what Dan was saying was true.

"In the first place," said Dan. "someone should stay here in case she tries to contact you. So if you want to go get the God damn paper, Kodak should stay here. Second, it's after 3:00 A.M. We won't be able to check out those garage sales until morning. Third, there are a lot of people who don't advertise garage sales in the paper. They just put a fuckin sign in the driveway or on the main road somewhere. So I suggest that as soon as you get that paper, you come back here and get a good night's sleep because if you don't hear from Nickel by the morning, God forbid, you're going to need some sleep so you can think with a clear head. We're going to have a lot of territory to cover and very little time to do it in. DO YOU GET MY DRIFT?"

The reality of what Dan was saying stung Bobby to his senses. He smiled at Dan. "Now I know why they made you Sheriff of Lake County."

CHAPTER 34

Nicole felt sluggish when she awoke. It was dark. Pitch black. Her head throbbed with pain. When she tried to touch it she realized at once that she was bound and could not move and then she remembered where she was. She tried to scream but the tape over her mouth muffled her cries. Her body began to quiver, not just from fear but from the cold. She was naked and lying on a dirt covered floor. She twisted and squirmed to free herself but it was useless. In frustration she began to cry. Suddenly she heard the sound of a dead bolt being thrown back and the creaky hinges of a door as it swung open. She could not see or hear anything, but she knew he was there. He was coming for her. "Bobby!" she tried to callout. "Please, Bobby . . . ." Then she felt a hot hand on her shoulder and she cringed in terror.

CHAPTER 35

Bobby sped to downtown Lake Forest. The main street was empty at such an early hour. He spotted a line of newspaper dispensers in front of the corner drugstore. The car lurched to a halt as Bobby threw the transmission into park before he had come to a complete stop, and he was out and running before the car settled at the curb. He dropped a handful of coins on the ground as he groped in his pocket for thirty-five cents. When he was sure he had gotten the right paper he jumped back in his car and headed home. "Home." He thought. It was his home now. Their home. As the cool early morning air rushed by his head he thought of her and what they had become to each other.

He was driving the car she bought for him as a surprise. And what a surprise it had been. They had been at the Chicago Yacht club having dinner after one of their days out on Big Mac. As they left and were walking through the parking lot, Bobby had admired the cherry '62 Buick Skylark convertible and had remarked to her about what a beauty it was. He told her that he had owned one like it in his youth and had loved it. A week later she presented the car to him. She refused to tell him how she had got the car.

He saw no for sale sign on it and when he pressed her, she had responded with a Mae West imitation: putting a hand behind her head, tilting her nose high in the air, and putting the other hand on her swinging hips as she said. "When I'm good, I'm very good. And when I'm bad, I'm even better!"

And shopping! She had taken him shopping at Northbrook Court. He had resisted going shopping for clothing but did it to please her. He'd had a great time as he spent more money on his wardrobe in that one day than he earned in an entire month from the city of Chicago. Just thinking about her made his heart leap.

As he pulled into the driveway, he half expected to see her car parked in its usual place. He wanted her to be safe inside the house, laughing with Kodak over their silly fears. But her car wasn't there. And when he shut off the engine he did something he hadn't done in many years. He prayed.

When he finally went into the house the expression on Kodak's face told him that she hadn't called. There was no news from her. They got down to work laying out the two newspapers on the dining room table and looking for the missing pieces and the garage sales she had planned to go to. Once they had finished that task there was little else they could do before morning so they went to bed.

Bobby slept very little. The bed linen smelled of her.

Her perfume. Her skin and hair. He clung to her pillow as if clinging to life. Her life. His dreams were unsettling and frightening although he couldn't remember what they were upon awakening. But the ominous feeling he got from them clung to him.

Finally, it was daybreak. He went to the kitchen shook the coffee pot and plugged it in. Nicole had always prepared it for the next day, right after breakfast, by filling it with fresh water and newly ground coffee. She hadn't failed him this morning. He stood there for a few moments and watched it perk. His mouth was dry as if he had a hangover though last night he'd had little to drink. The house was quiet and his footsteps echoed when he walked on the cool Mexican tile. He entered the front room and turned on the radio to break the deafening silence. Kodak soon came walking into the kitchen, still sleepy-eyed.

"What hit me?" He said rubbing his head. "I feel like shit."

"Good morning to you too." Bobby replied. "I know how you feel. Coffee will be ready in a few minutes. Grab a seat."

Bobby walked out to the front steps and got the two newspapers. He threw them down in front of Kodak. He was in no mood to read them.

"Holy shit!" Kodak exclaimed. "In the excitement I forgot all about this." He showed Bobby an article on the front page. The article was headed:

POLICE INSPECTOR CASH REINSTATED

After reading the article to him, Kodak got up and went outside to his car. When he came back into the kitchen he handed Bobby his gun and shield. "Welcome back Inspector."

As Bobby looked at his badge, he had a strange feeling, as if he were seeing it for the first time. "Thanks." was all he could say. The phone rang breaking the awkward moment.

Bobby grabbed the phone. His disappointment was apparent in his voice as he said, "Oh Hi Dan. Any news?"

"Nothing yet. But I've got ten men checking on the ads the Morton girl circled. We're sweeping the area of her disappearance as well as the area the Emerson woman disappeared in. I had a dozen copies of Nickel's photo printed. It's exactly what we planned yesterday, only more. We'll find her Bobby. I promise you.

"I know that Dan. I appreciate everything you're doing.

"Did you get a copy of the paper she had yesterday?"

"Yes. I got one from town last night. Kodak and I are going split the garage sale ads. We can check them out faster that way."

"Well, good luck and God bless. Keep me posted. If you or Kodak need any help, call."

After they hung up, he poured a cup of coffee for himself and one for Kodak. It was strong and black. Instead of drinking their usual three or four cups they were ready to go after just one. There was no time to waste. Bobby took three of the ads and gave the other three to Kodak. They each took a picture of Nicole with them. Before they parted in the driveway they stopped as if to say something further to each other. But only looks of determination covered their faces as they patted each other on the shoulder. They headed in opposite directions.

Bobby looked at the first ad. It read:

GARAGE SALE Fri.-Sat.-Sun.
8AM to 4PM
Cockatoo to collectibles
No early birds!
637 Hill Drive, Forest Lake

Bobby hopped over to Half Day Road and headed west. It was easy to find the town of Forest Lake, but he had to stop at what appeared to be a general store to find out where Hill Drive was. The woman behind the counter was extremely helpful and showed him on a street map how to get there.

Hill Drive was on the outskirts of town. A hand made garage sale sign was stuck in the lawn beside the driveway at number 637. Bobby pulled in and walked up to the front door of the house. He didn't see a door bell so he knocked. He got no response, so he knocked harder and longer.

"I'm coming! I'm coming!" He could hear someone yelling from inside. A woman wearing a robe and round pink curlers in her hair opened the door a little. "For Christ's sake," she said, "do you know what time it is? It's not even 7:00 A.M. yet. When I said no early birds, I meant it!" She slammed the door in Bobby's face.

He knocked again. "Open the door ma'am. Police!"

She opened the door, only more sheepish this time.

"Since when is it against the law to have a garage sale?"

"As far as I know, ma'am, it's not. I'm investigating a missing person who might have come to your sale yesterday." Bobby held up one of the pictures he had found of Nicole and his grandmother. He pointed to Nicole. "I'm looking for this woman. Have you seen her?"

The woman studied the picture carefully and then shook her head. "Can't say I have, but I wasn't here all day yesterday. My daughter was, though. Maybe she saw her."

"Where's your daughter, ma'am? I'd like to talk to her."

"She's sleeping." Then disgustedly, she added. "As usual. Wait just a minute and I'll get her."

A teenage girl soon came to the door rubbing her eyes.

Bobby showed her the picture. She hadn't seen Nicole either.

"Are you positive? I know you're sleepy, but take a good look."

It didn't help. The girl hadn't seen her.

"Fuck!" Bobby said under his breath as he got back in his car. He looked at the next ad.

GARAGE SALE
Sat.-Sun. 8AM-5PM
Many Antiques, Knick-Knacks
Furniture, etc.
738 County Line Road, Barrington

Bobby sped to that address, ignoring all speed limit signs. He spotted the house. A garage sale sign was posted by the driveway. He pulled in. A heavyset woman in her late sixties was tinkering around items spread out on tables in the open garage when Bobby walked up.

"Ma'am? He said, coming up behind her. She jumped back and held her hand to her chest.

"Land sakes! You just scared the devil out of me!" She smiled at Bobby as she caught her breath. "What's a nice young man like you looking for so bright and early this morning? Maybe I'll just happen to have it." She had a twinkle in her eye.

"I'm just looking for some information, ma'am." He took out his badge and showed it to her. "I'm looking for this woman. I have reason to believe she might have come here yesterday. Did you see her? Bobby handed the woman the picture.

"Why land's sake, yes! Nicole."

Bobby's heart did a flip-flop.

"I remember her well. She and I talked for the longest time about the restaurant business. You see, when I was a young woman, many years ago, I owned a restaurant in Arlington Heights by the race track, before my husband and I retired and moved out here. Well, when my husband died, I took up antiquing. Used to go all over the country picking up pieces of this and that. I'd sell most of it at auctions and shops, and sometimes, a real good piece to a Michigan gallery."

"But what about Nicole?" Bobby said. He was trying to contain his impatience.

"Well, let's see. She must of got here about noon.

Yup, it was noon. I remember cause I was sitting in the garage eating a tuna fish sandwich. I offered her some, but she declined. Anyway, she mentioned that she was opening some restaurant. Had a fancy French name if I remember right. She was looking for decorations to hang on the walls. That's when we got to talking. She's a very nice young woman."

"Do you remember what time she left here and did she happen to say where she was going?" Bobby had his fingers crossed.

"I don't know. We probably chatted for a good half-hour before she left. She bought a small, light blue Limoge vase and a King's Rose dinner plate from me. The plate was worth about three hundred dollars but she was so nice I gave it to her for only two hundred. She loved the pattern. Said it—"

"Did she say where she was going? Bobby interrupted her.

"No. I don't remember her saying anything. Only that she'd have to keep looking until she found all the stuff she needed."

Bobby thanked the old woman for her help and then drove down the driveway. Well, at least he knew that Nicole had been there. He recalled what Dan had said about garage sales not always being advertised, so he drove up and down roads in the immediate vicinity, stopping at places with garage sale signs. He questioned several people, but no one else had seen her, not even at the third garage sale ad in the paper.

He pulled into a gas station to phone Dan to find out whether anyone had come up with anything. They hadn't but Dan was encouraged when Bobby told him he had found someone who'd seen Nicole. He told Bobby he would call in some of his men to concentrate on the Barrington-Long Grove area.

Bobby got back in his car. He sat for a while trying to decide what direction Nicole might have taken. Then he realized that she probably went toward Long Grove, where she planned to attend the auction later that afternoon. With nothing else to go on, he followed his hunch.

There were several possible routes she could have taken to get to Long Grove. Bobby came up with nothing on the first route he drove. He found very few garage sales on the way, and no one at any of them had seen her. The second route he chose had a few more garage sales but he got the same results, nothing. He was about to turn around and head in another direction when he saw a Garage Sale sign on the other side of the cross roads. It was almost hidden by weeds and was up farther in the driveway than most other signs. He pulled into the gravel driveway and stopped. The words "GARAGE SALE" were written in a child-like scrawl. A big, run-dawn-looking farmhouse set back well off the road was half hidden by immense trees that surrounded it. Bobby drove slowly up the driveway and saw another sign printed in the same child-like scrawl: IN THE BARN, with an arrow pointing toward the dilapidated barn behind the house. A dirt ramp led to the top floor of the barn, which was sitting on a hill, making it seem as if the first floor of the building was buried in the ground. He got out of the car and slowly walked up the incline and through the doorway. Old bales of hay were scattered around the plank flooring amidst junk of all kinds—weathered horse collars, antique copper tubs, picture frames, fasteners, old tools, all kinds of odds and ends of every description. Bobby didn't hear the soft footsteps coming up behind him.

"Can I help you?" An unseen voice said.

Bobby jumped, spun around and came face to face with a dark-eyed, bald-headed man.

"You gave me a start." Bobby said. "I didn't hear you." Bobby studied the man in front of him. He didn't have a beard or hair, but Bobby suspected this could be Beltzer. He had the right build and was about the right age but there was something about his eyes. Like Charles Manson eyes. Wild yet blank. Unfeeling. That was the best way he could describe them. He wished he could see the man's left upper arm, to check for the tattoo, but this man was wearing a long-sleeved shirt.

"I'm just looking." Bobby said casually. "My girlfriend collects all this crap. Antiques, I mean. I thought if I found something special I'd get it for her birthday. Her birthday's Wednesday." he lied.

"Help yourself." the bald man said. "If you got any questions, just ask."

Bobby nodded his head. He hoped if this man was Beltzer he wouldn't recognize him. Bobby had been on television and in the papers a lot lately. But today dressed as he was, in jeans and a plaid shirt, and driving his Buick, he hoped he didn't look like a cop.

His gut instinct told him this was his man. This was John Beltzer. He moved around the barn floor, looking at various pieces of junk, but not ever completely turning his back on the man. He pretended to be interested in the trash littering the floor and made casual comments as he inspected them.

The sun was high in the sky now and shone brightly through the holes in the roof of the barn. Pigeons cooed high in the rafters above nervously flapping their wings. Particles of hay floated in the air tickling Bobby's nostrils. A long table had been set alongside one of the weathered walls of the building. Bobby walked over to the table and casually picked up various articles all the time keeping the man in his vision. He could feel the piercing stare from the cold black eyes behind him. Suddenly, an object glistening in the sunlight caught his attention. He moved towards it and picked it up. It was a buffalo nickel encased in silver. He turned it over. "I love you, Bobby." it said.

He felt a sharp pain go through his chest. His heart pounded. It was Nicole's nickel. The nickel he had given her. He saw that the chain was broken and could imagine Beltzer ripping it off her long, lovely neck. It took every fiber of strength he had to put the nickel back down, turn and say nonchalantly to the man. "Well, I don't see anything she might like. Guess I'll have to look somewhere else."

He approached John Beltzer faking a smile. There was no doubt now. Bobby's body tensed as he got closer to him. Casually he pretended to walk by him then with the reflexes of a boxer he pivoted and threw a crushing right cross to Beltzer's face. The blow broke Betzer's nose. The spray of blood splattered them. Beltzer fell to the floor like a sack of flour. Bobby picked him up and hit him again, this time in the stomach. Beltzer moaned, doubled over and fell back down to the floor. Bobby grabbed him again and pulled him to his feet in the process ripping off Beltzer's shirt. He saw the large tattooed anchor on Beltzer's arm. He hit him again. And again.

Bobby couldn't contain his rage. He grabbed Beltzer by the throat. "Where is she?" he screamed tightening his grip on Beltzer's throat. "Where is she? Tell me or I'll rip your God damn windpipe out of your throat!"

Barely able to talk Beltzer mumbled, "Down below. In the milkhouse." Bobby pulled him to his feet with such force he lifted his feet off the ground. Pulling out his revolver Bobby snarled between clenched teeth. "Show me." He shoved Beltzer hard in the back with the barrel of his gun.

Beltzer stumbled on his way to the small concrete block building that was attached to the backside of the barn on the downstairs level. It was well concealed. Only part of the roof could be seen from where Bobby stood. The wooden door on the scanty building was closed. It had a hasp with a locked paddock on it. Bobby didn't bother waiting for a key. He threw Beltzer against the door with such strength the impact burst the door off its rusty hinges and it and Beltzer fell into a heap on the hard, cold floor.

Bobby couldn't see Nicole anywhere in the small building. "Where?" He shouted at the semi-conscious Beltzer. Beltzer pointed to the shallow rectangular concrete pit which used to be used for cooling milk. Bobby walked over to the pit and looked down. He could see the outline of a body buried beneath coarse dark gray granules. A delicate hand and long dark hair protruding from the makeshift grave were the only clues to the beautiful woman hidden beneath it. He could tell by the color of the skin that he was too late. That she was dead. That he would never feel the warmth of her body next to him again. Bobby's heart rose to his throat. Tears stung his eyes. He let out a scream.

"Noooo . . . . His anguish echoed through the barnyard. The pigeons scattered in fear. "No . . ." Bobby screamed, over and over. His anguish turned to hate as he looked back at Beltzer.

"What did you do to her, you bastard? What the hell is that stuff?" He yelled at Beltzer, the veins protruding from his neck. Beltzer grinned. Blood caked his teeth.

"It's lime." He said proudly. "It incinerates flesh."

His chuckle sickened Bobby. Suddenly Bobby couldn't breath. Couldn't catch his breath. He turned and stared at Beltzer who was still lying on the floor. He walked over to him and picked him up. He glared into Beltzer's cold, black eyes. The vicious empty eyes of a great white shark. Flat and yet shiny. He grabbed Beltzer by the throat lifting him up. Beltzer gurgled from the pressure. Bobby fixed his eyes on Beltzer's face. He was seething inside, losing control. Then he hit him. He hit him harder than he had every hit anyone in his whole life. Not as a cop but as a lover. As a victim. Beltzer flew into the concrete wall behind him. His eyes bulged open as he violently hit the wall. Then as if in slow motion he hung suspended in midair against the wall before finally crumbling onto the milkhouse floor.

Bobby walked over to the pit. He stared down at the woman he loved. The man in him wanted to grab her, hold her, but the cop in him knew he mustn't. It could mean the difference between Beltzer frying in the chair or possibly getting off on a technicality. Agony wrenched his body. Shakily he sat himself down on the edge of the pit.

"Why didn't I tell you I loved you when I had the chance." he said into the pit but not looking into it. "Why did we have to have this fight this morning? Why did I have to be so God damn stubborn about the baby!" He smashed his fist against the concrete unaware of any pain as his knuckles were stripped of flesh. "The baby." he said to himself looking down into the pit. They are both dead now. He would not get a second chance. He has lost everything that mattered to him.

It was the sound of John Beltzer's moans as he regained consciousness that brought Bobby's mind back to him. To what he had done to Nicole. He looked at the revolver in his hand and over at Beltzer. He got up and walked over to Beltzer. He knelt down beside him. Beltzer was whimpering now. He saw the look in Bobby eyes and knew what he was thinking. Bobby put the barrel next to Beltzer's head and cocked the trigger. His eyes were glassy and his body felt hollow and empty. Lightly he applied pressure to the trigger and began to squeeze. He wanted him dead. But as much as he wanted to he could not. If he did he would be no better than Beltzer. No better than the killer sniveling beside him.

"Please. Please." Beltzer whined. "Don't kill me."

Bobby uncocked the gun and was about to put it away when he said, "Fuck it!" and struck Beltzer squarely against the side of his head, knocking him unconscious. He stood up and looked down at the pathetic excuse of a man that lay in front of him. He reached for his handcuffs and realized that Kodak had forgotten to give them to him so he hunted around until he found some bailing wire to tie Beltzer's hands and feet with.

Listlessly Bobby walked down the lane to the farmhouse and used the phone to call Dan. When he was done, he walked back to the milkhouse and waited.

It seemed like an eternity before Dan and Kodak arrived escorted by an entourage of patrol cars. They spotted Bobby sitting quietly under a tree and walked up to him.

"Bobby . . . ." Dan began. "I can't tell you how sorry I am. I know how much you loved her. I loved her too." Dan's voice cracked. "She was like a daughter to me. You know that."

"Yeah, Bobby." Kodak said, "I'm sorry . . . ." He wanted to say more but he knew his words were inadequate.

"Where is she Bobby?" Dan said wiping his eyes with the back of his hand.

Bobby pointed to the small building behind him. Dan motioned to a waiting team of investigators to begin their work. He and Kodak followed. Beltzer was just regaining consciousness as they walked in the building. His face was covered with dried blood and deep purple splotches. Dan pulled him roughly to his feet and yelled to one of the officers present. "Read the bastard his rights!" Then slowly he walked over to where the photographer was taking pictures and looked down. Through a trembling voice he said, "Kodak go get a couple of guys and get her the hell out of there." Kodak nodded meekly.

"But chief, we're not . . . ." One of the investigators started to say, but knew from his superior's look that his protests were falling on deaf ears.

As Kodak walked past Beltzer flung his tied body at Kodak and screamed, "That fucking bastard is going to pay. You hear me. I'm going to sue you for police brutality! I'm going to have your badges. You're not going to get away with this. Do you hear me?" His mouth was foaming. Kodak grabbed him by his shirt, looked him cooly in the eyes and brought a hard right knee up to the center of Beltzer's groin. Beltzer yelped in pain. Kodak released the grip on Beltzer's shirt and he crumbled and fell to the floor. Kodak looked down at him and said quietly. "Now shut the fuck up or next time I'll really hurt you."

Kodak walked outside. Bobby was still sitting under the tree. Kodak motioned for the ambulance attendants to go inside the milkhouse and retrieve Nicole's body. When Bobby saw them he stood and pointed a threatening finger at them. "You be gentle with her. You hear me?"

They both nodded. "And another thing. I want her taken to the Cook County Morgue and turned over to Walt Barber, the M.E. No one else. Got that?"

"But we're in Lake County . . . ." They started to protest until they saw Dan approaching shaking his head indicating they were to do what Bobby was telling them. The two men walked towards the milkhouse. Dan put his hand on Bobby's shoulder. "Why don't you go home, Bobby. We'll take care of this. Go home."

Bobby didn't answer. He shrugged his shoulders and began to walk down the lane where he left his car. He hadn't gotten very far when he heard one of the officers yell. "Chief, we've found a woman back here and she's alive!"

Bobby turned. His eyes focused on two policeman coming out of a shed at the rear of the property assisting a woman between them. Her head was hanging down as they helped her walk. Her long dark hair covered her face. One of officer's had covered her with his jacket concealing her nakedness.

She was too far away for Bobby to see clearly. "It couldn't be." he thought. "Or could it?" He began to walk, then run towards her. Not believing what he was seeing, he shouted. "Nicole." Slowly she lifted her head. It was her. It was Nicole. He rushed to her. She saw him coming and smiled. Tears stained her dirt covered face. When he reached her he took her from the policemen as carefully as helping a baby bird that had fallen from its nest. He scooped her up into his waiting arms. "Bobby . . . ." she said weakly.

"Shhh . . . ." he said. "Everything's going to be all right. Everything is going to be just fine."

Postscript

"BIG MAC" sliced through the dark blue water of the Atlantic, leaving a large, bubbling wake in her path. The skyline of Key West was visible on the horizon. Bobby, at the helm, felt relaxed. He thought of how far away Chicago was and how glad he was to have left it. He had no regrets about resigning from the Chicago Police Department. There was more to life than chasing killers. He took a deep breath of the fresh salt air and smiled contentedly.

"Lunch is ready." Nicole said as she came up the ladder to the bridge. Her face was beaming. She looked so beautiful that Bobby's heart raced at the sight of her. Her olive complexion was deeply tanned and her long dark hair had bright auburn streaks running through it. She was thinner than she had been but other than that she seemed totally recovered from her ordeal with Beltzer and the trauma of the miscarriage of their baby.

"Is my Captain hungry?" She asked coyly. Bobby shut off the engines and motioned for her to come sit in his lap.

"I'm hungry enough," he said wrapping his arms around her. "but food is the last thing I have on my mind right now."

And it was.